Dear parents, caregivers, and educators:

If you want to get your child excited about reading, you've come to the right place! Ready-to-Read *GRAPHICS* is the perfect launchpad for emerging graphic novel readers.

All Ready-to-Read *GRAPHICS* books include the following:

★ **A how-to guide to reading graphic novels for first-time readers**

★ **Easy-to-follow panels to support reading comprehension**

★ **Accessible vocabulary to build your child's reading confidence**

★ **Compelling stories that star your child's favorite characters**

★ **Fresh, engaging illustrations that provide context and promote visual literacy**

Wherever your child may be on their reading journey, Ready-to-Read *GRAPHICS* will make them giggle, gasp, and want to keep reading more.

Blast off on this starry adventure . . . a universe of graphic novel reading awaits!

Judge Kim
and the Kids' Court

The Doggie Defendant

written by **Milo Stone, Shawn Martinbrough,** and **Joseph P. Illidge**

illustrated by **Christopher Jordan**

Ready-to-Read *GRAPHICS*

Simon Spotlight

New York London Toronto Sydney New Delhi

SIMON SPOTLIGHT
An imprint of Simon & Schuster Children's Publishing Division
1230 Avenue of the Americas, New York, New York 10020
This Simon Spotlight edition January 2023
Text copyright © 2023 by Shawn Martinbrough, Milo Stone, and Joseph P. Illidge
Illustrations copyright © 2023 by Christopher Jordan
All rights reserved, including the right of reproduction in whole or in part in any form.
SIMON SPOTLIGHT, READY-TO-READ, and colophon are registered trademarks of
Simon & Schuster, Inc.
For information about special discounts for bulk purchases, please contact
Simon & Schuster Special Sales at 1-866-506-1949 or business@simonandschuster.com.
Manufactured in the United States of America 1222 LAK
2 4 6 8 10 9 7 5 3 1
Cataloging-in-Publication Data for this title is available from the Library of Congress.
ISBN 978-1-6659-1967-8 (hc)
ISBN 978-1-6659-1966-1 (pbk)
ISBN 978-1-6659-1968-5 (ebook)

Cast of Characters

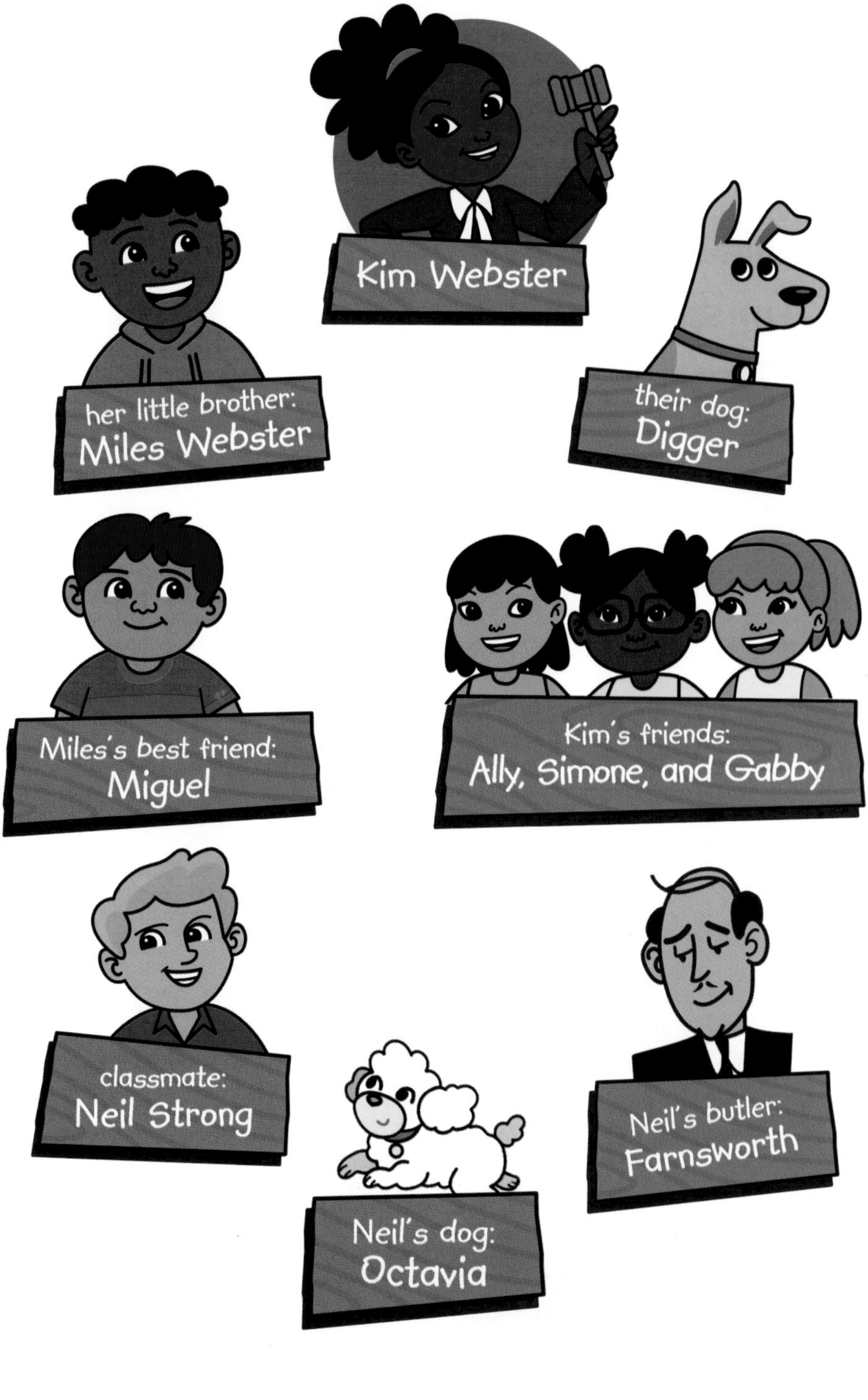
Kim Webster
her little brother:
Miles Webster
their dog:
Digger
Miles's best friend:
Miguel
Kim's friends:
Ally, Simone, and Gabby
classmate:
Neil Strong
Neil's butler:
Farnsworth
Neil's dog:
Octavia

This is Kim. She's here to give you some tips on reading this book.

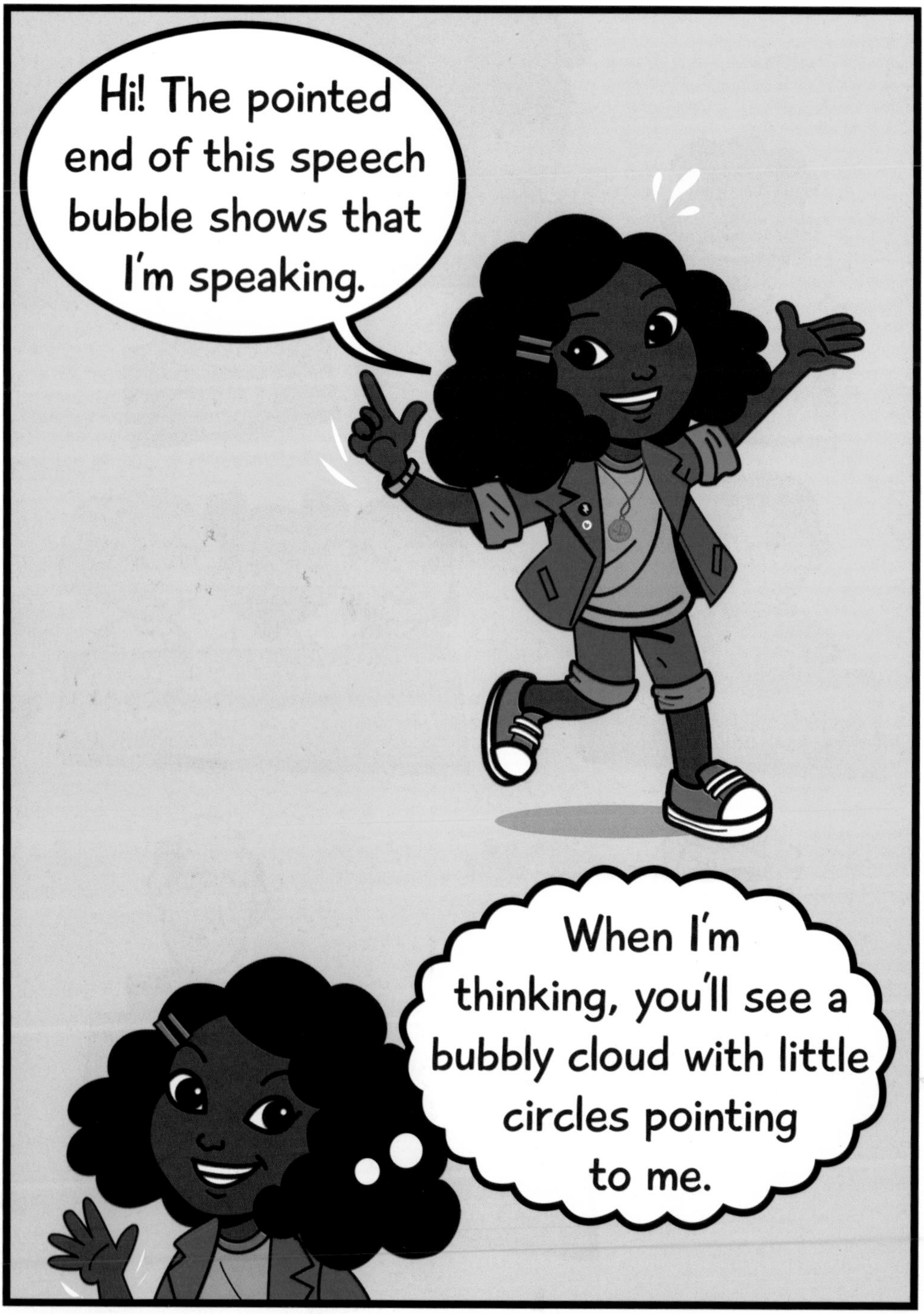
Hi! The pointed end of this speech bubble shows that I'm speaking.
When I'm thinking, you'll see a bubbly cloud with little circles pointing to me.

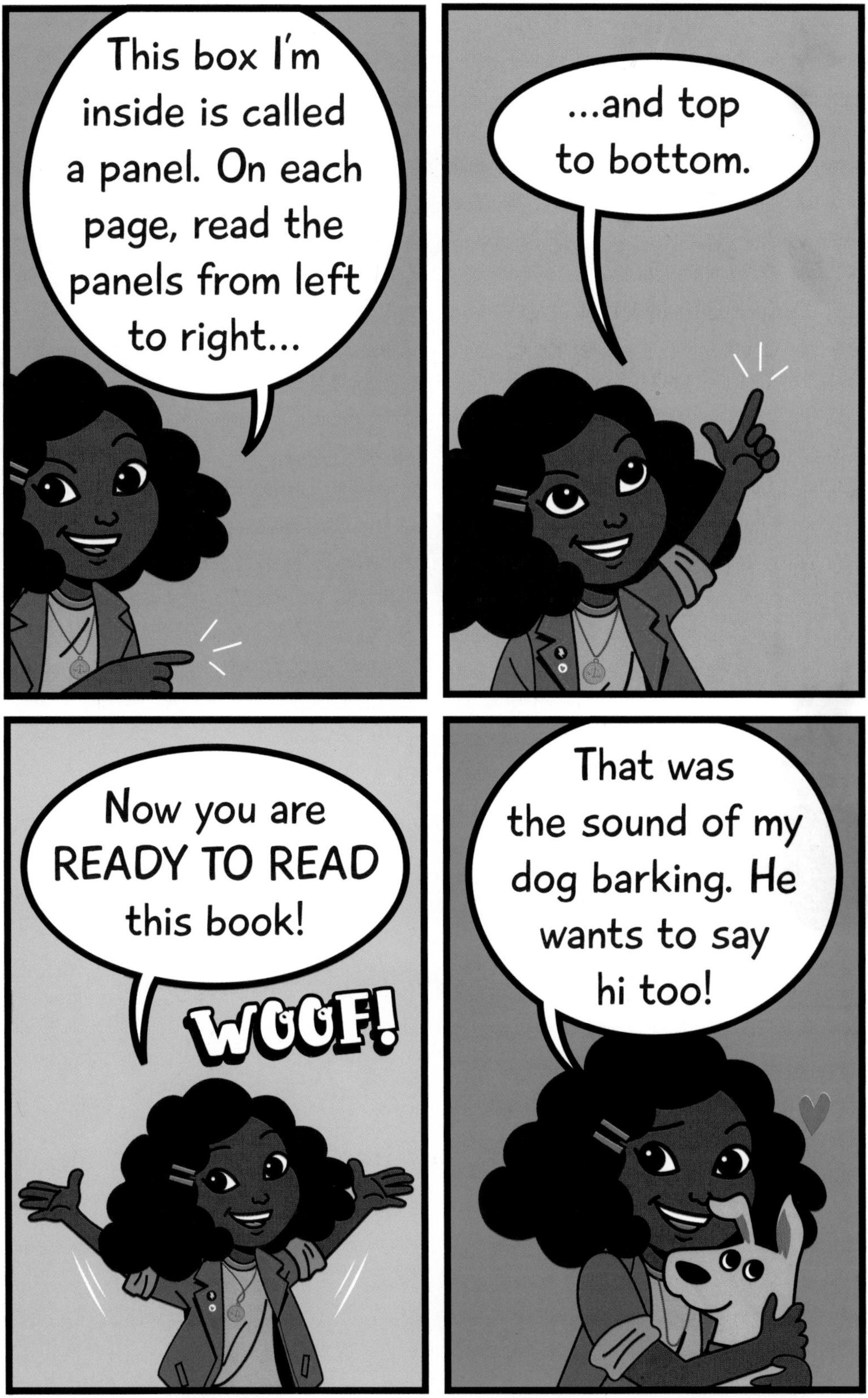
This box I'm inside is called a panel. On each page, read the panels from left to right...
...and top to bottom.
Now you are READY TO READ this book!
WOOF!
That was the sound of my dog barking. He wants to say hi too!

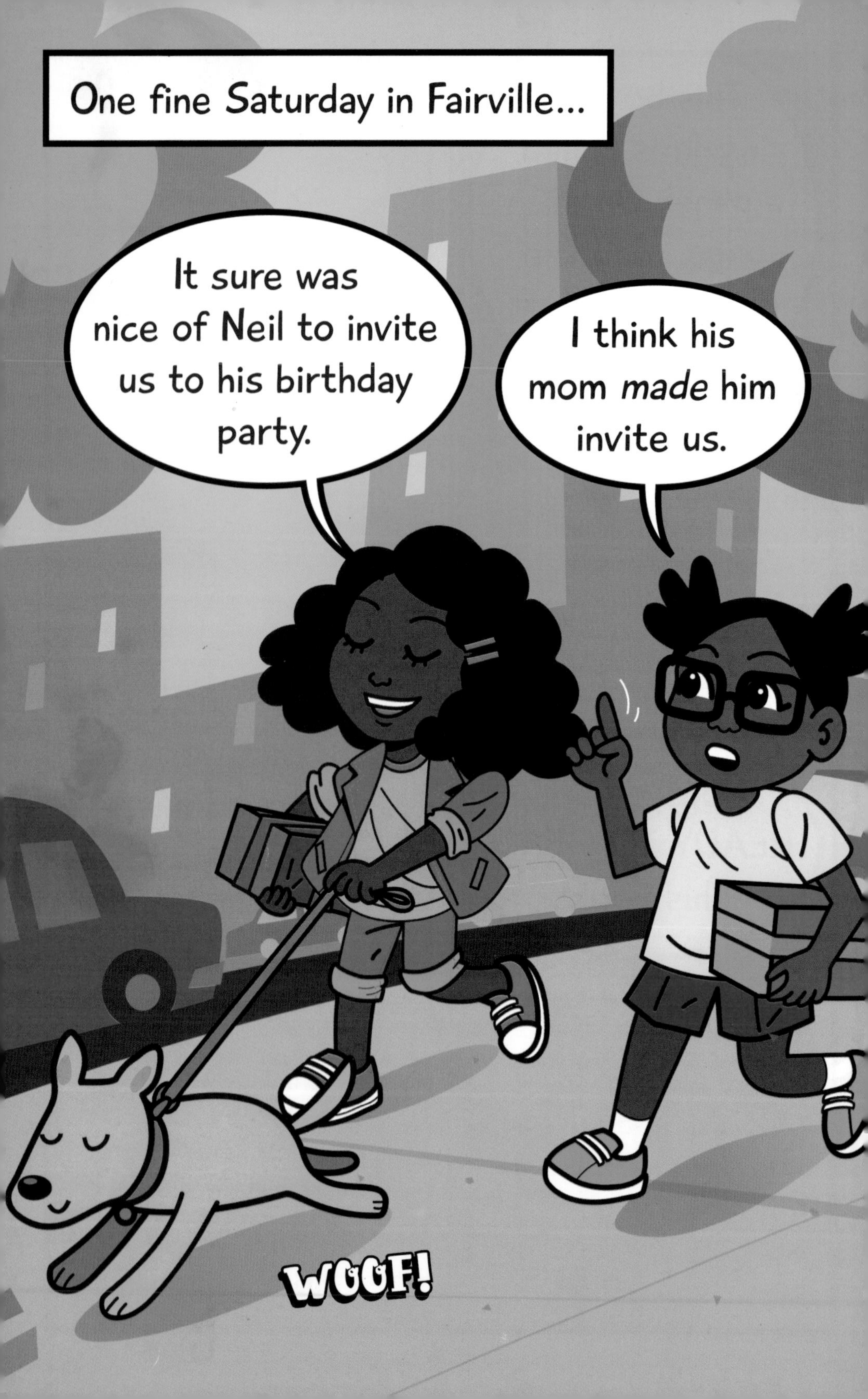
One fine Saturday in Fairville...
It sure was nice of Neil to invite us to his birthday party.
I think his mom *made* him invite us.
WOOF!

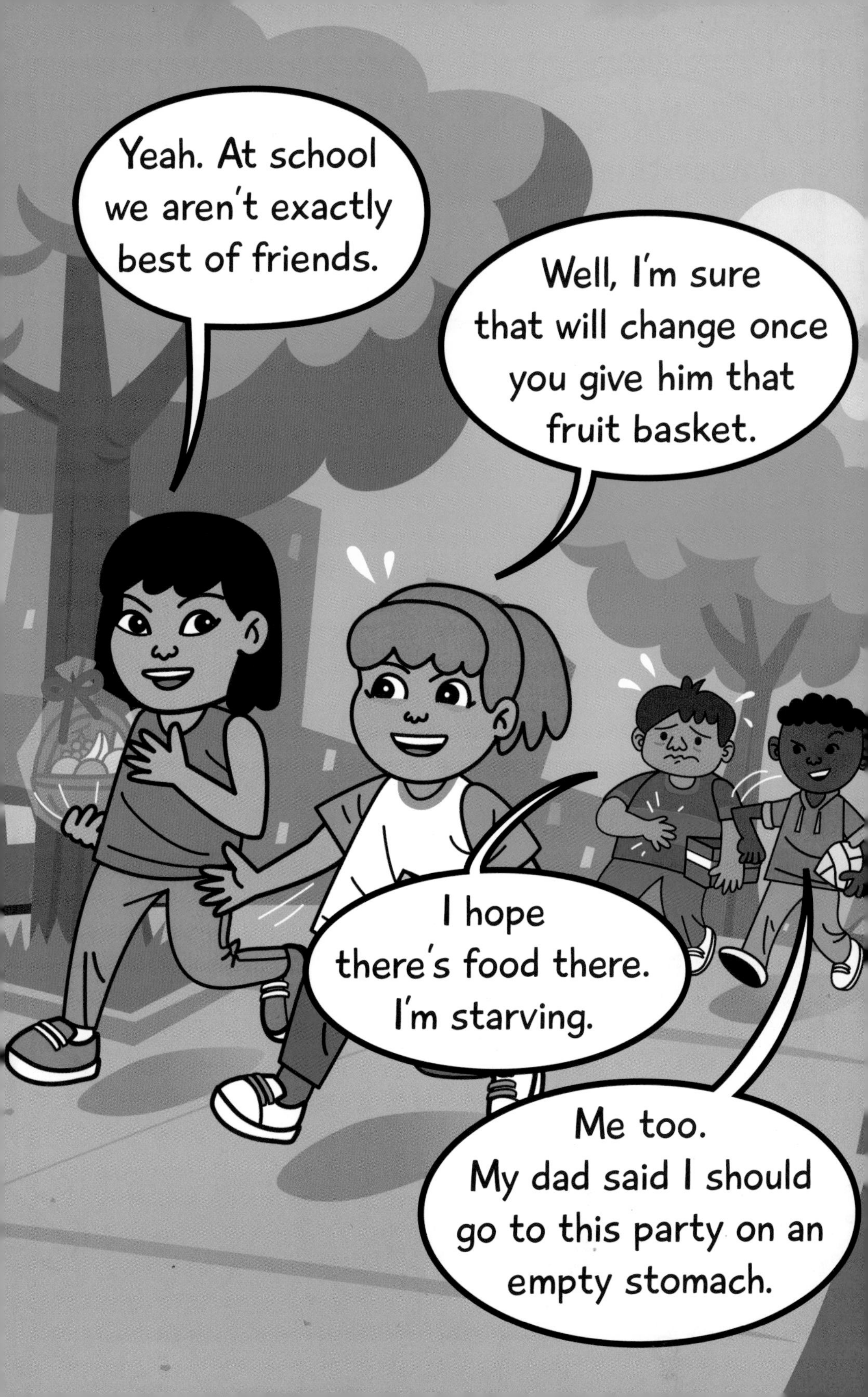
Yeah. At school we aren't exactly best of friends.
Well, I'm sure that will change once you give him that fruit basket.
I hope there's food there. I'm starving.
Me too. My dad said I should go to this party on an empty stomach.

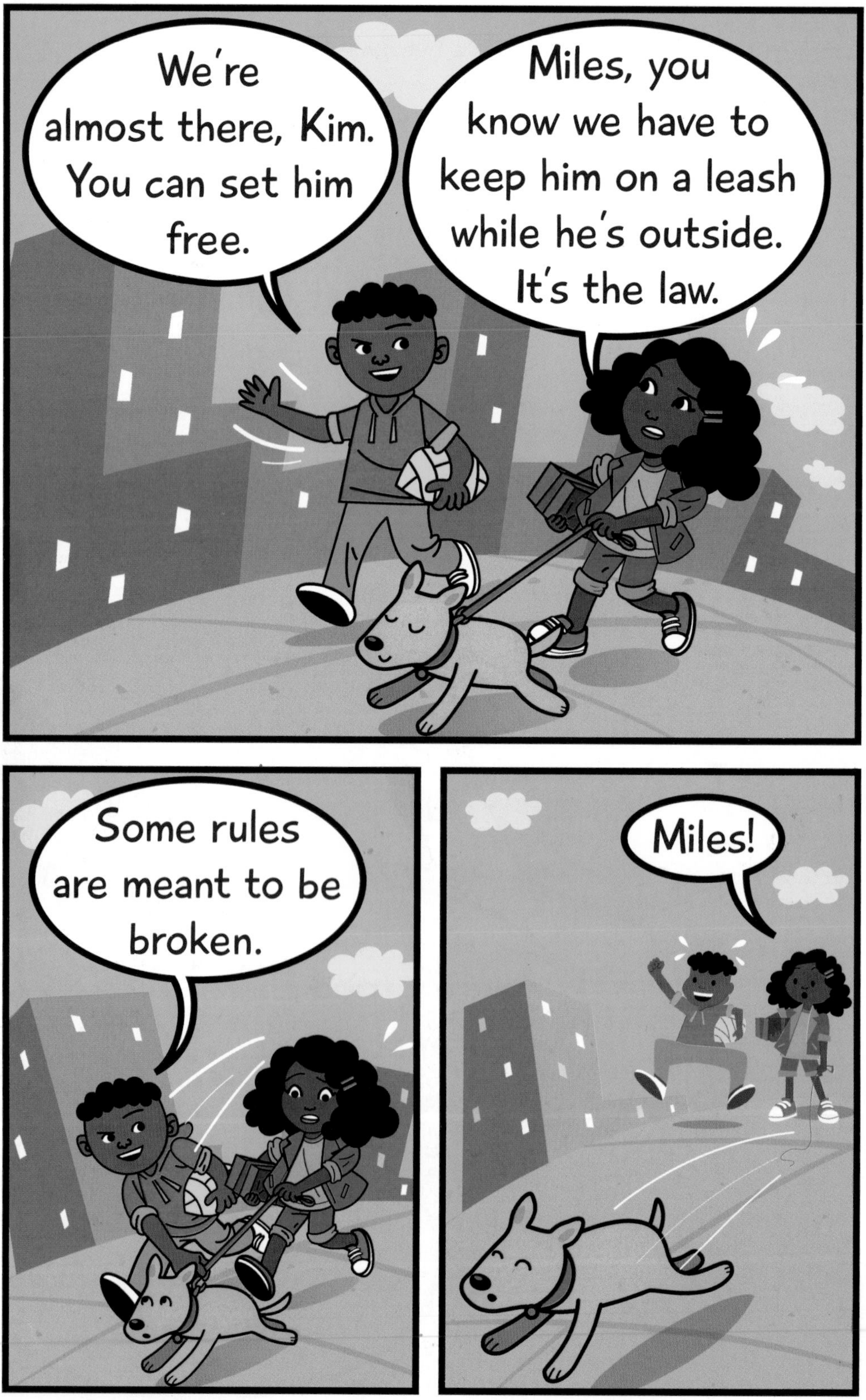
We're almost there, Kim. You can set him free.
Miles, you know we have to keep him on a leash while he's outside. It's the law.
Some rules are meant to be broken.
Miles!

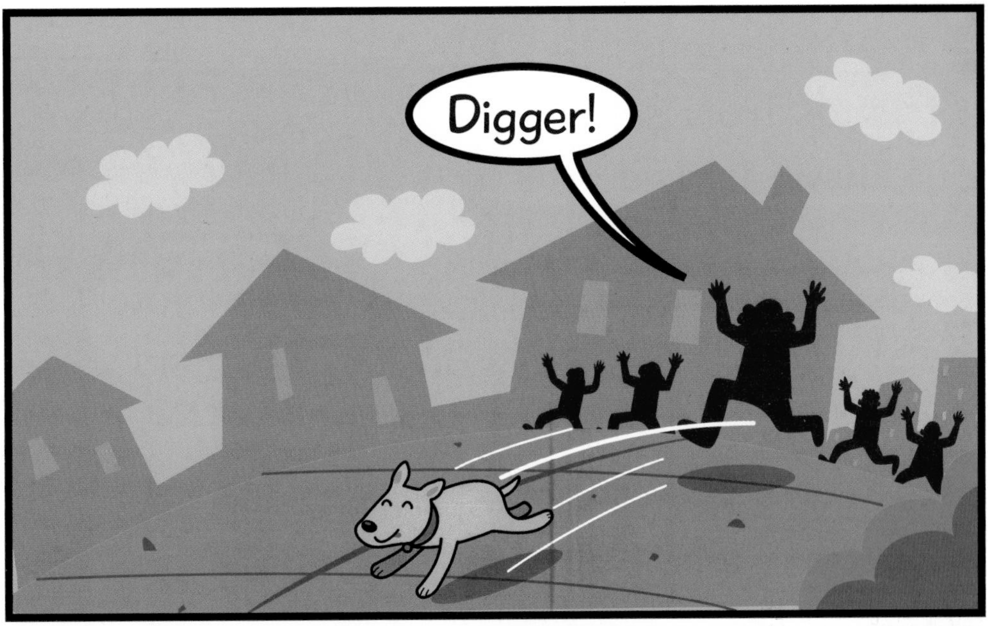
Digger!

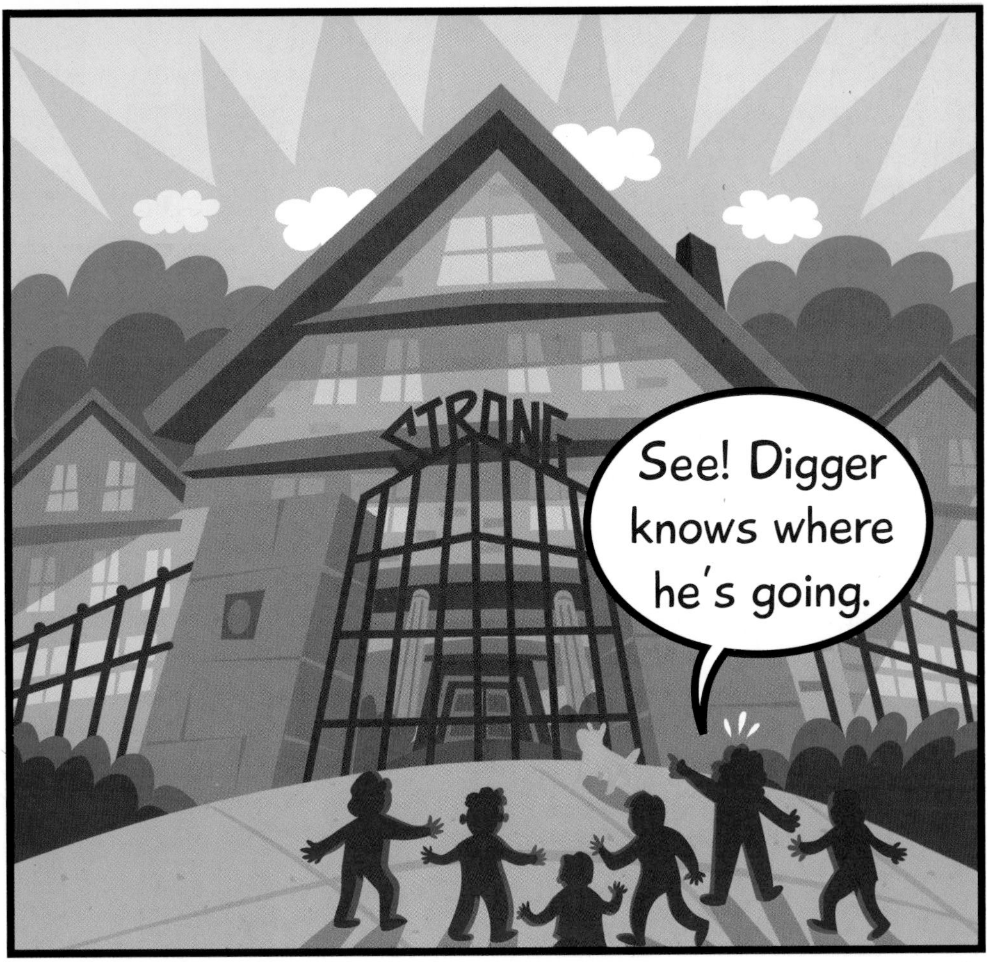
STRONG
See! Digger knows where he's going.

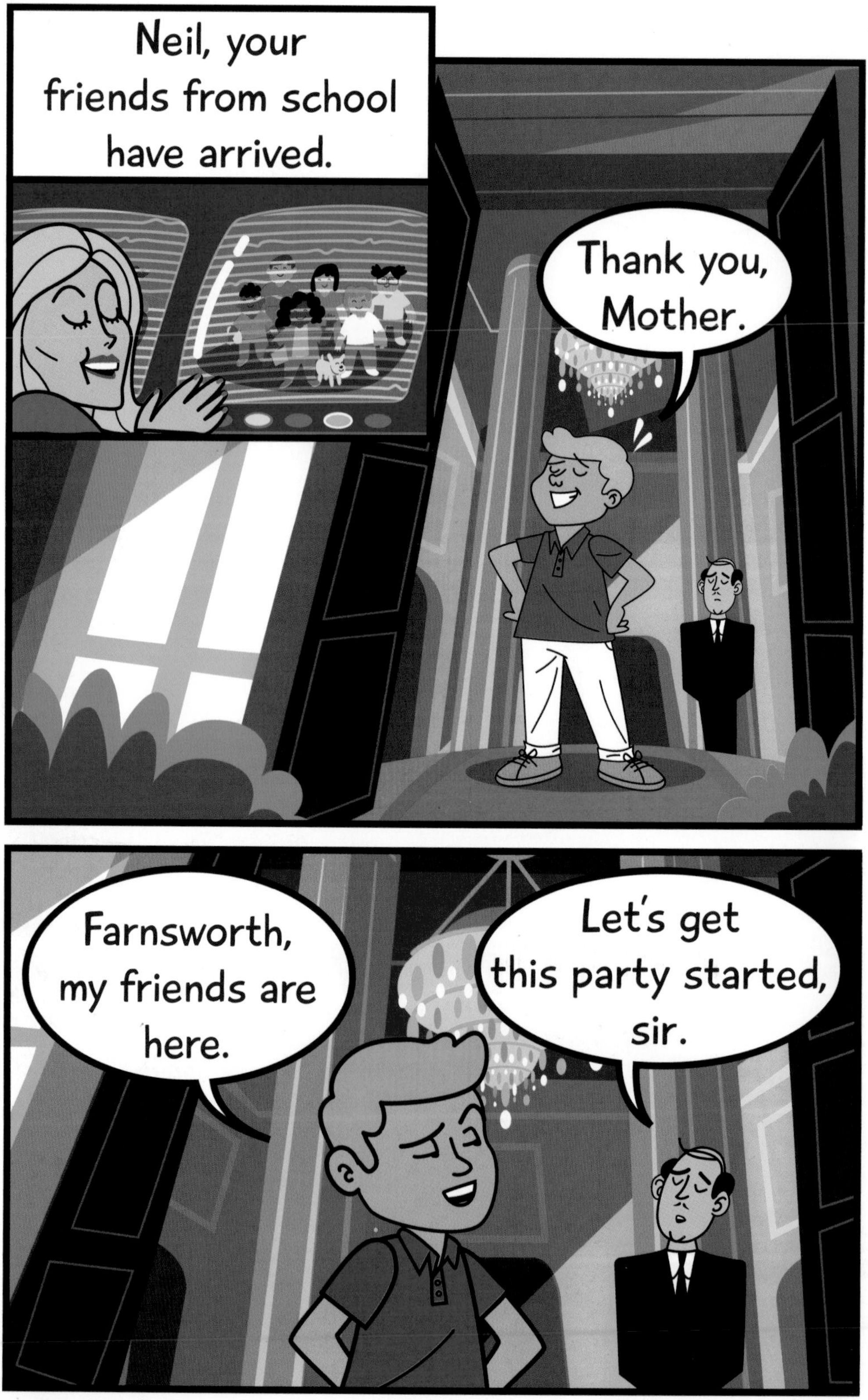
Neil, your friends from school have arrived.
Thank you, Mother.
Farnsworth, my friends are here.
Let's get this party started, sir.

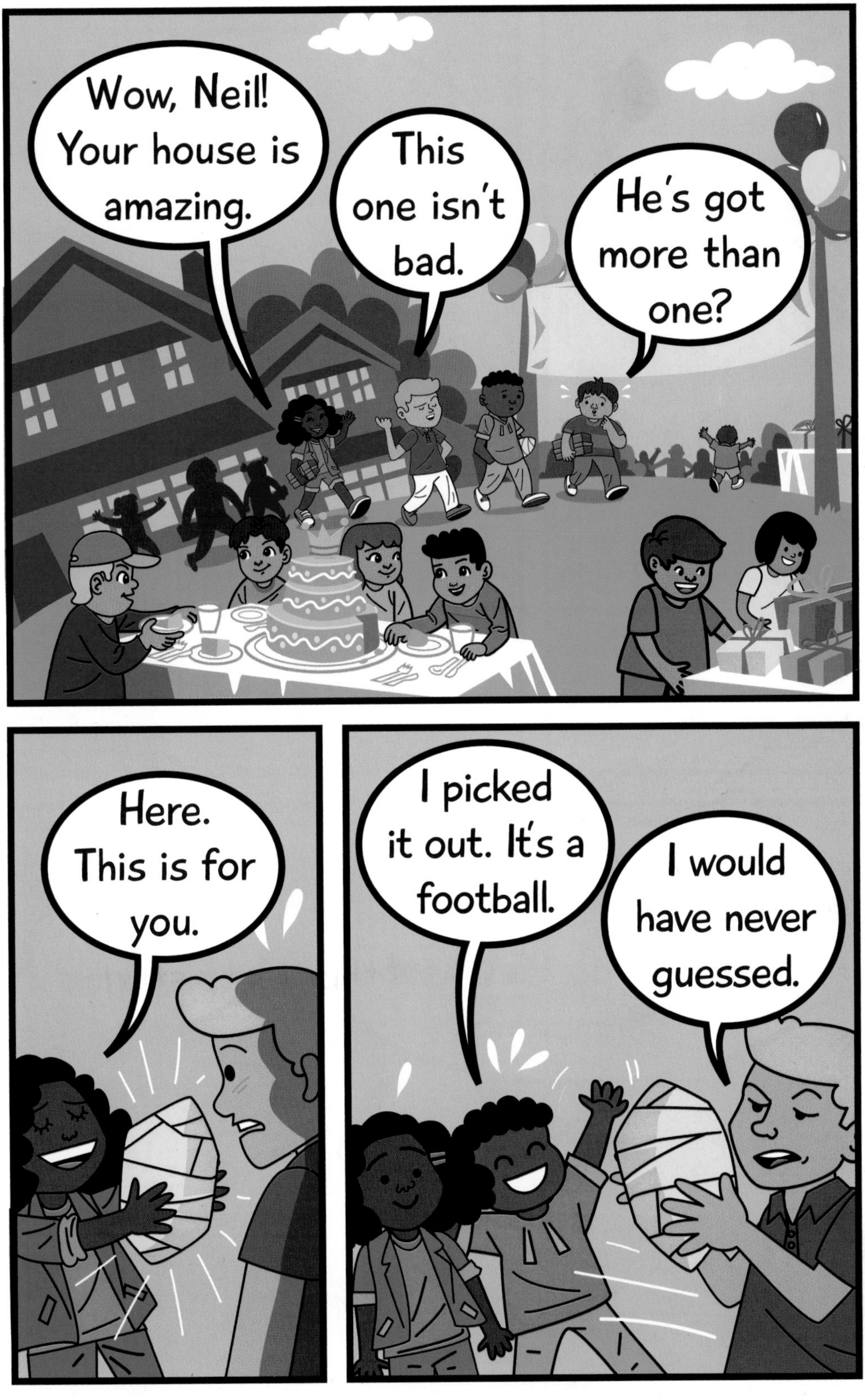
Wow, Neil! Your house is amazing.
This one isn't bad.
He's got more than one?
Here. This is for you.
I picked it out. It's a football.
I would have never guessed.

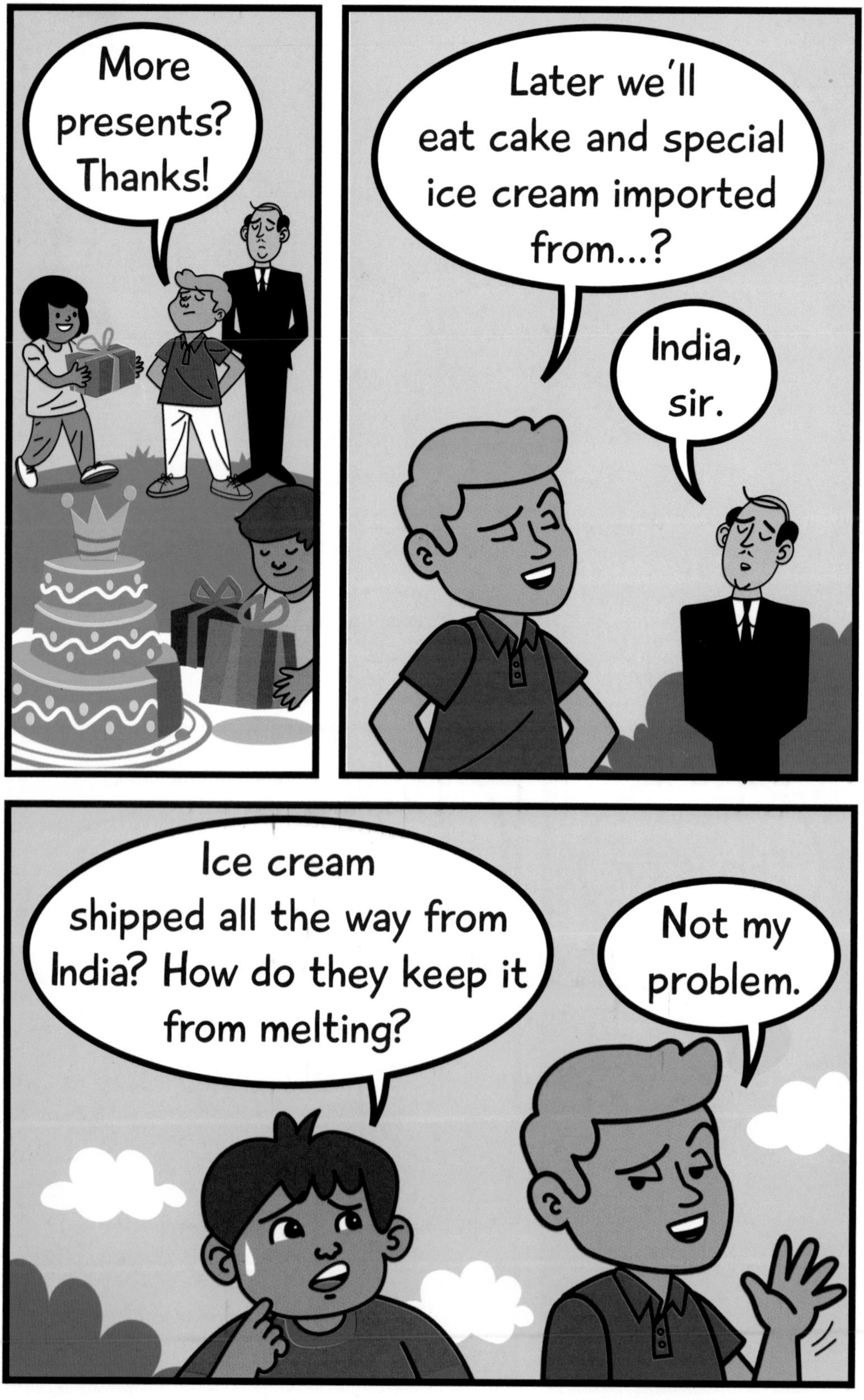
More presents? Thanks!
Later we'll eat cake and special ice cream imported from...?
India, sir.
Ice cream shipped all the way from India? How do they keep it from melting?
Not my problem.

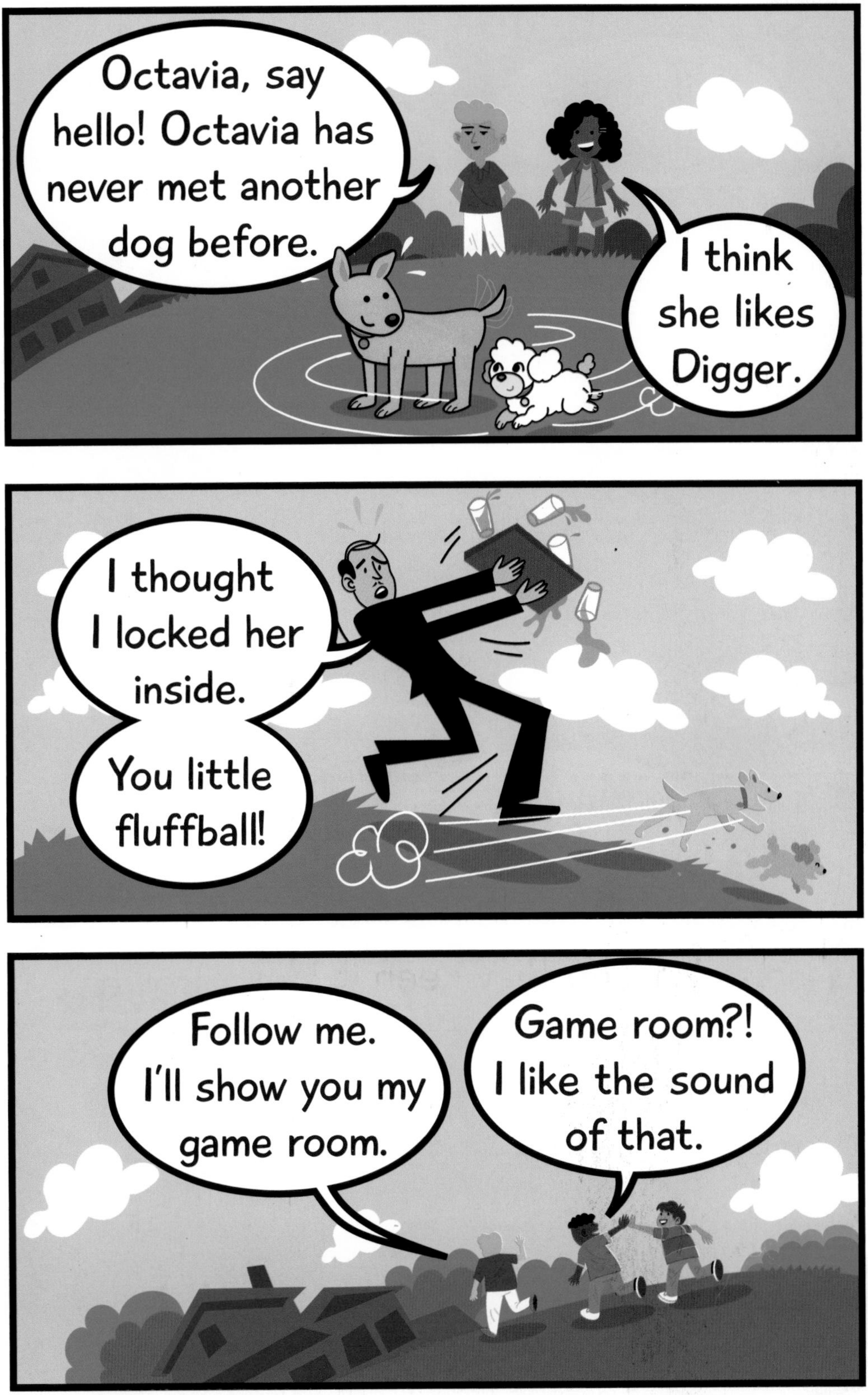

Octavia, say hello! Octavia has never met another dog before.
I think she likes Digger.
I thought I locked her inside.
You little fluffball!
Follow me. I'll show you my game room.
Game room?! I like the sound of that.

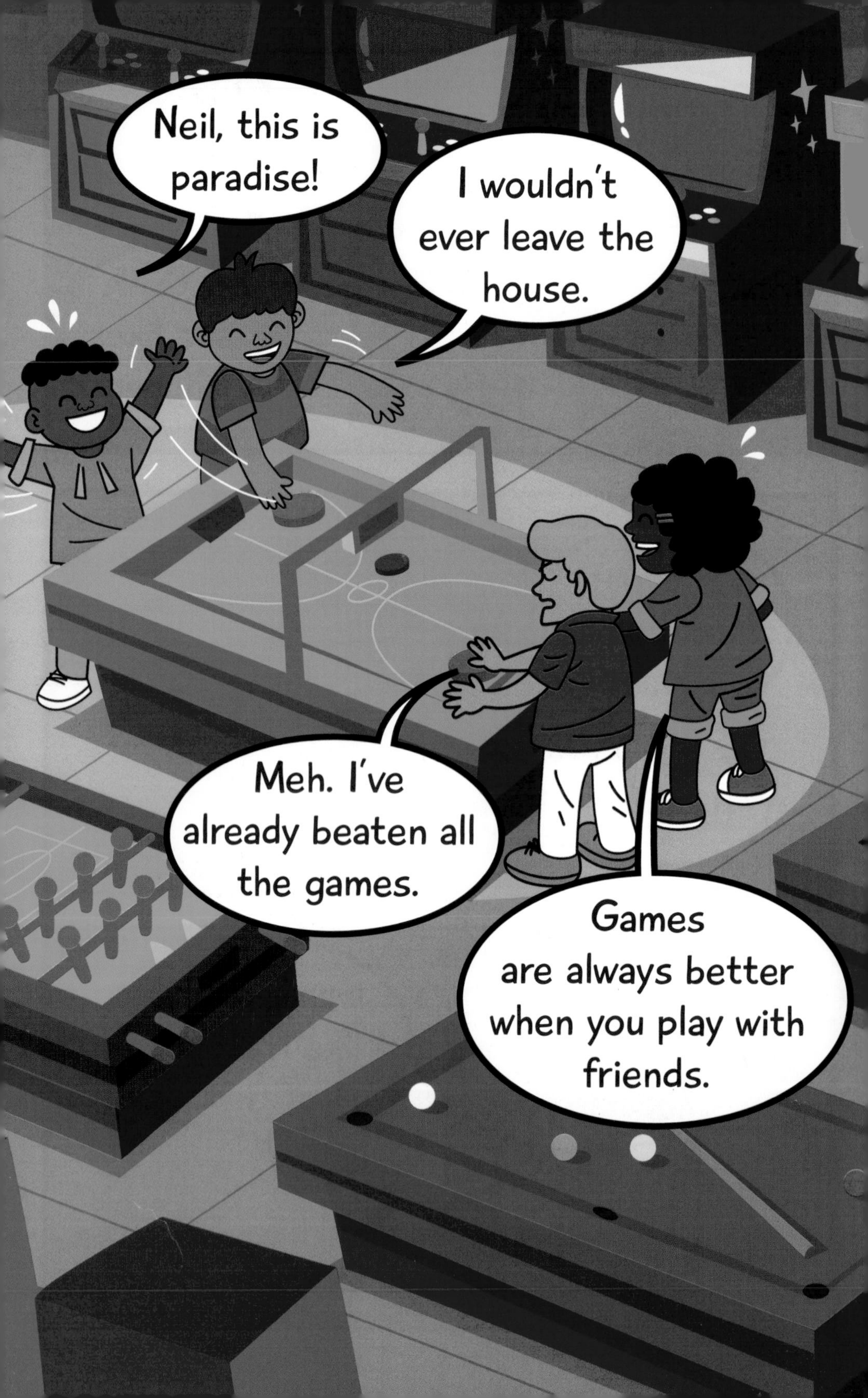
Neil, this is paradise!
I wouldn't ever leave the house.
Meh. I've already beaten all the games.
Games are always better when you play with friends.

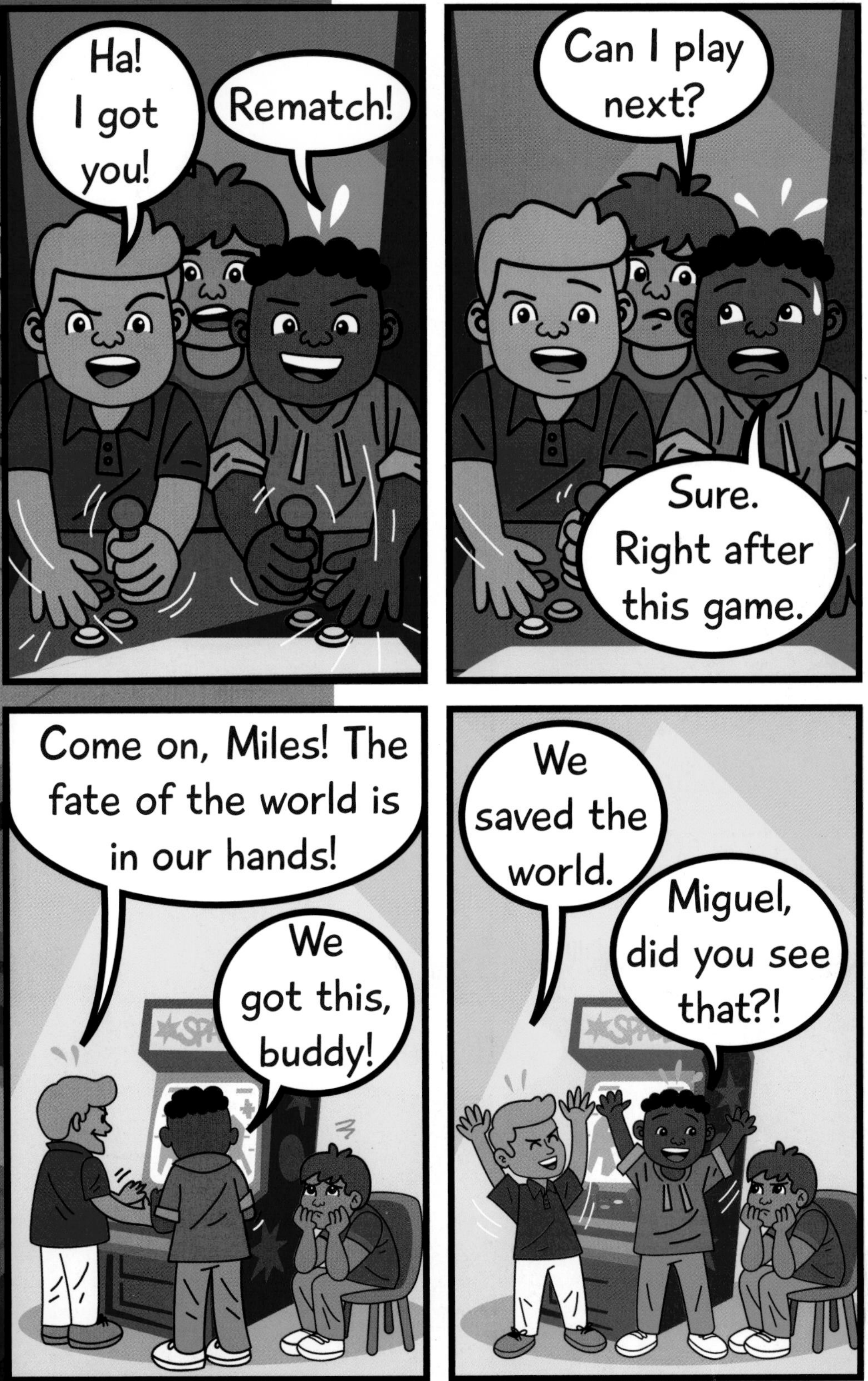
Ha! I got you!
Rematch!
Can I play next?
Sure. Right after this game.
Come on, Miles! The fate of the world is in our hands!
We got this, buddy!
We saved the world.
Miguel, did you see that?!

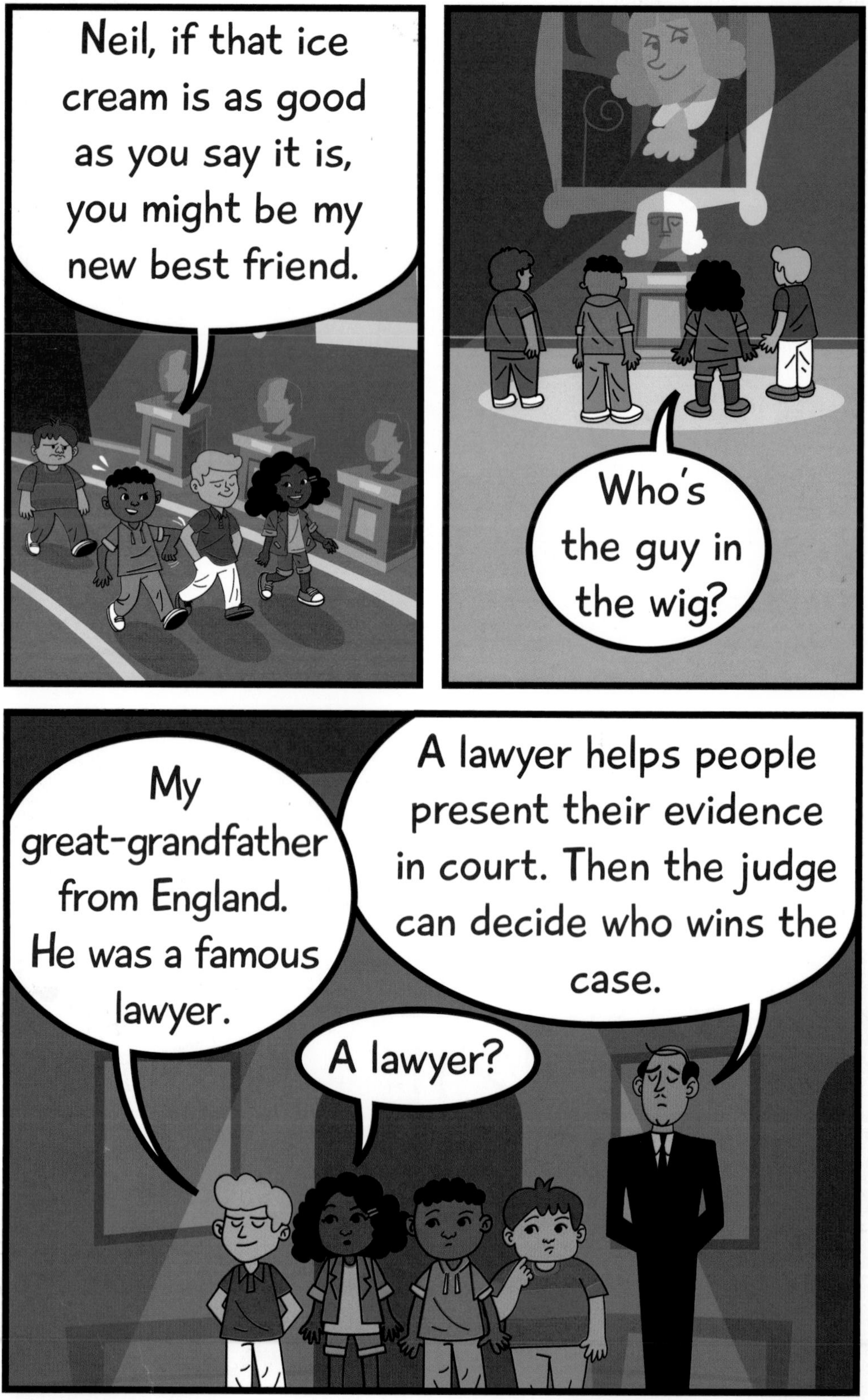
Neil, if that ice cream is as good as you say it is, you might be my new best friend.
Who's the guy in the wig?
My great-grandfather from England. He was a famous lawyer.
A lawyer?
A lawyer helps people present their evidence in court. Then the judge can decide who wins the case.

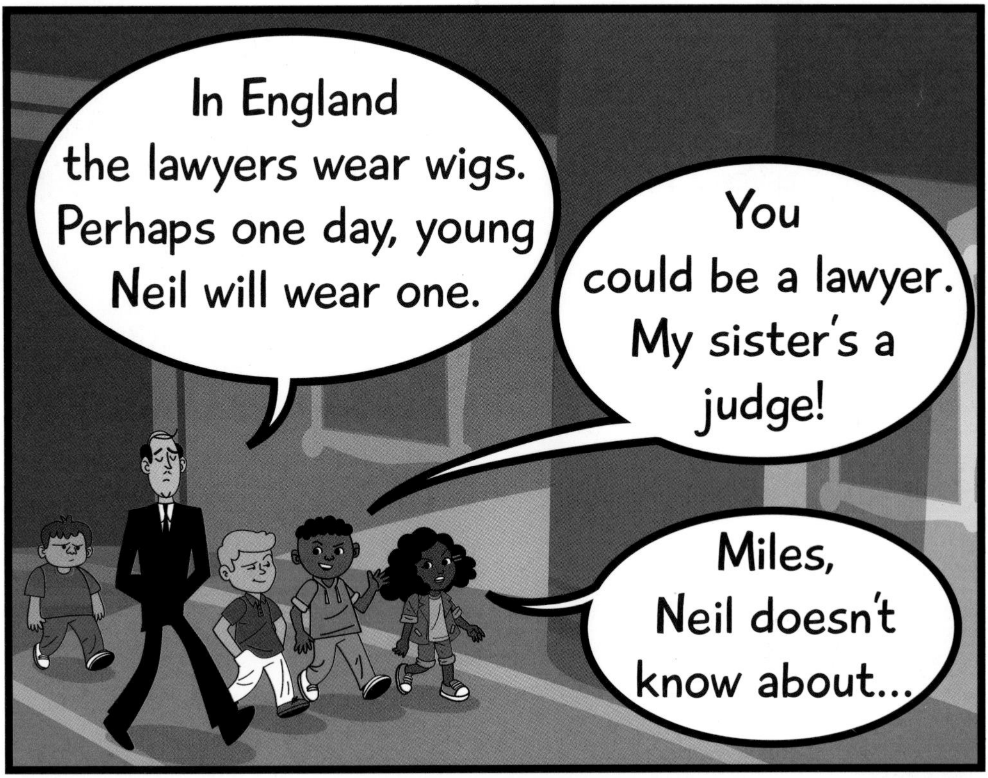
In England the lawyers wear wigs. Perhaps one day, young Neil will wear one.
You could be a lawyer. My sister's a judge!
Miles, Neil doesn't know about...

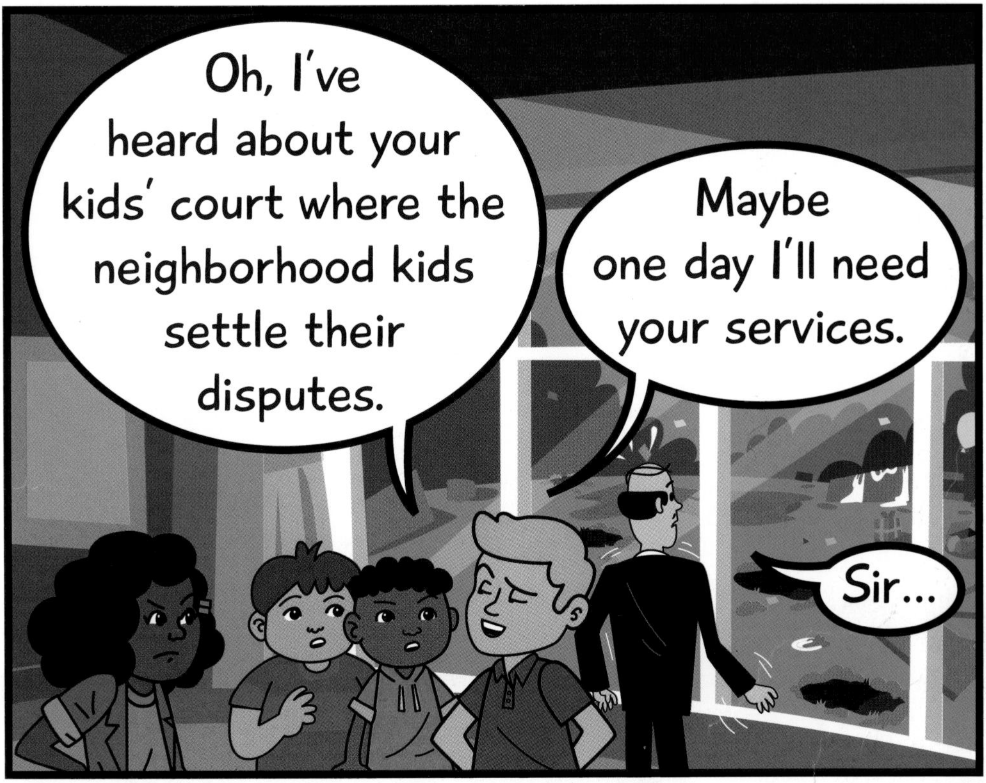
Oh, I've heard about your kids' court where the neighborhood kids settle their disputes.
Maybe one day I'll need your services.
Sir...

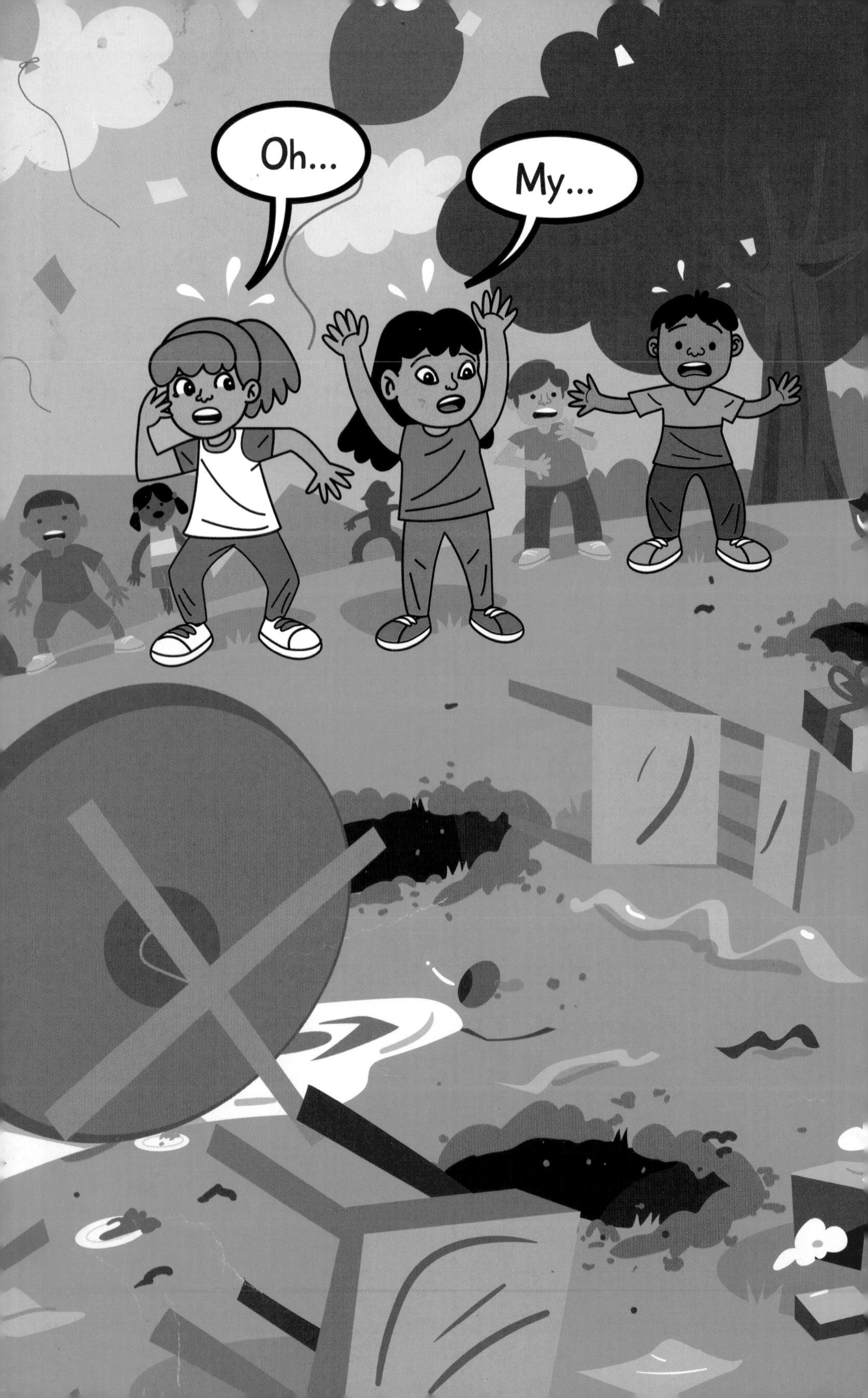
Oh...
My...

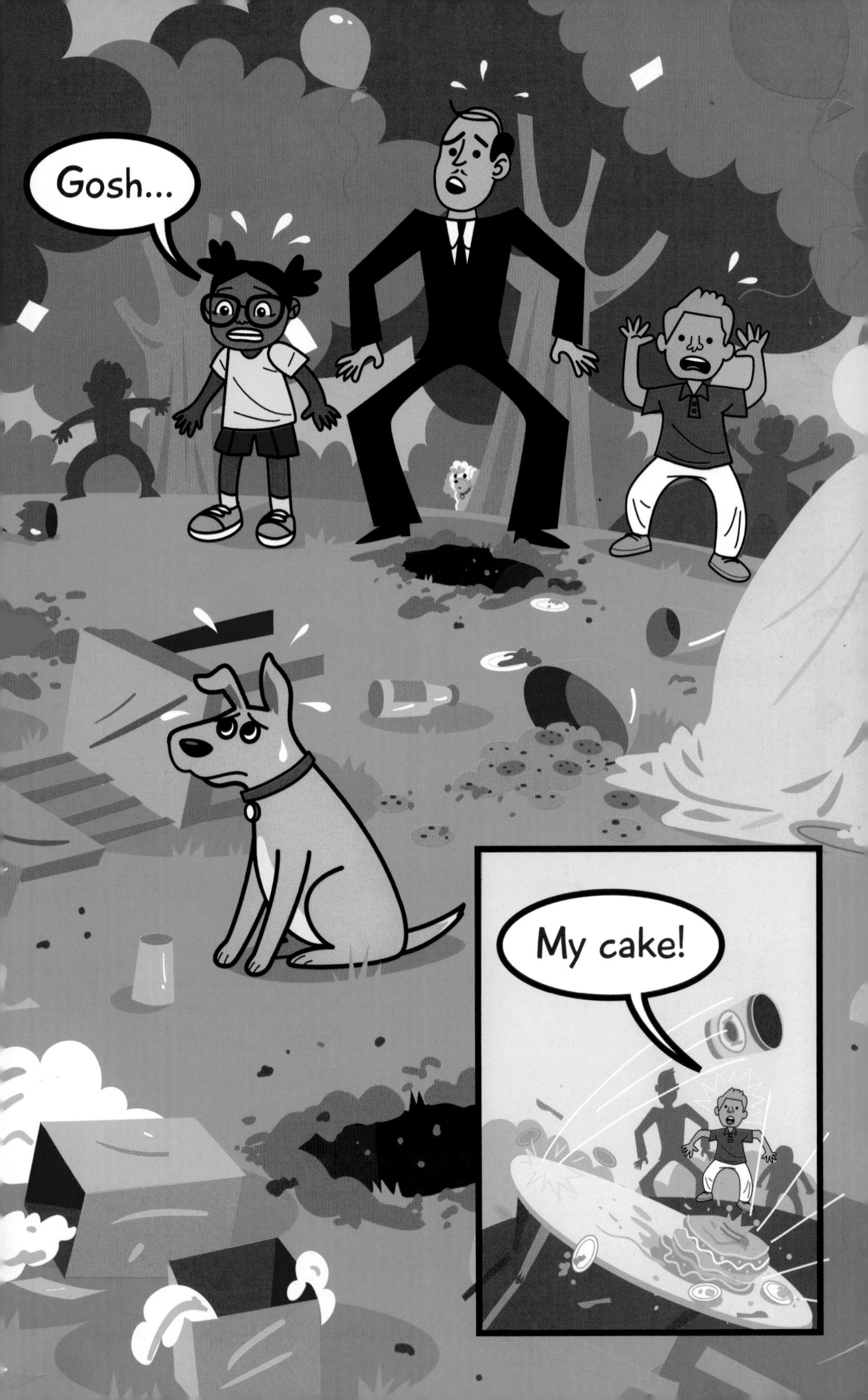
Gosh...
My cake!

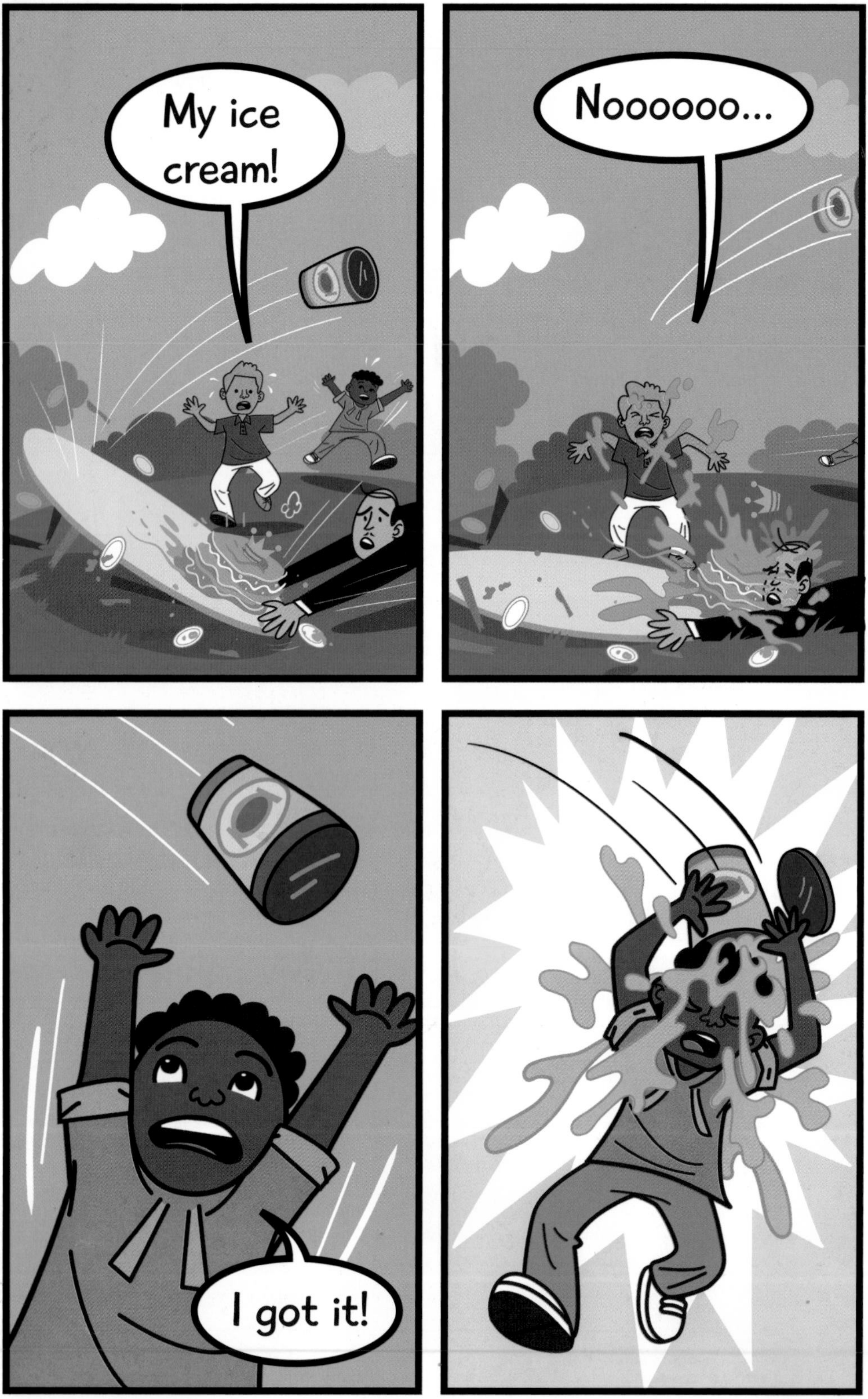
My ice cream!
Noooooo...
I got it!

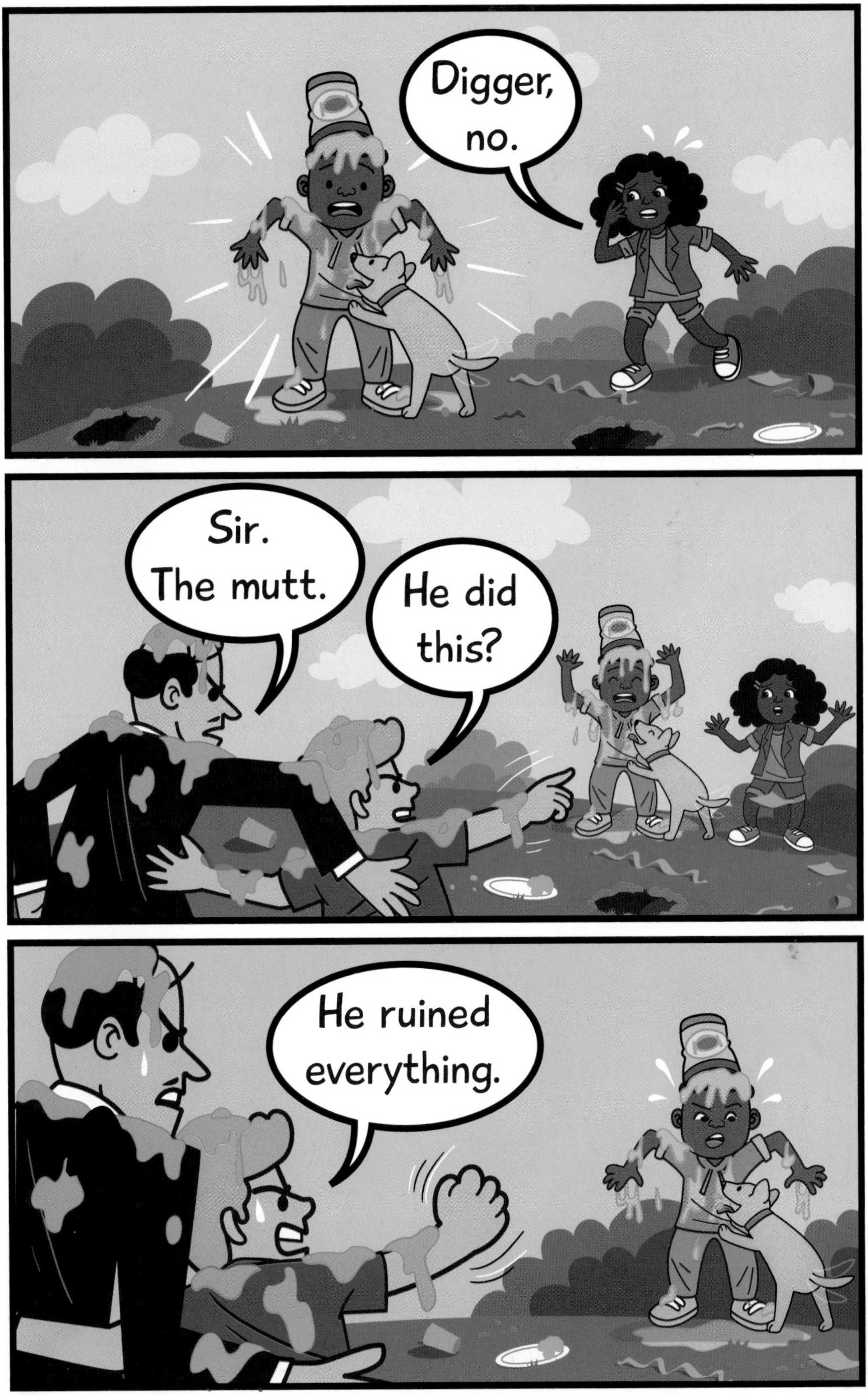
Digger, no.
Sir. The mutt.
He did this?
He ruined everything.

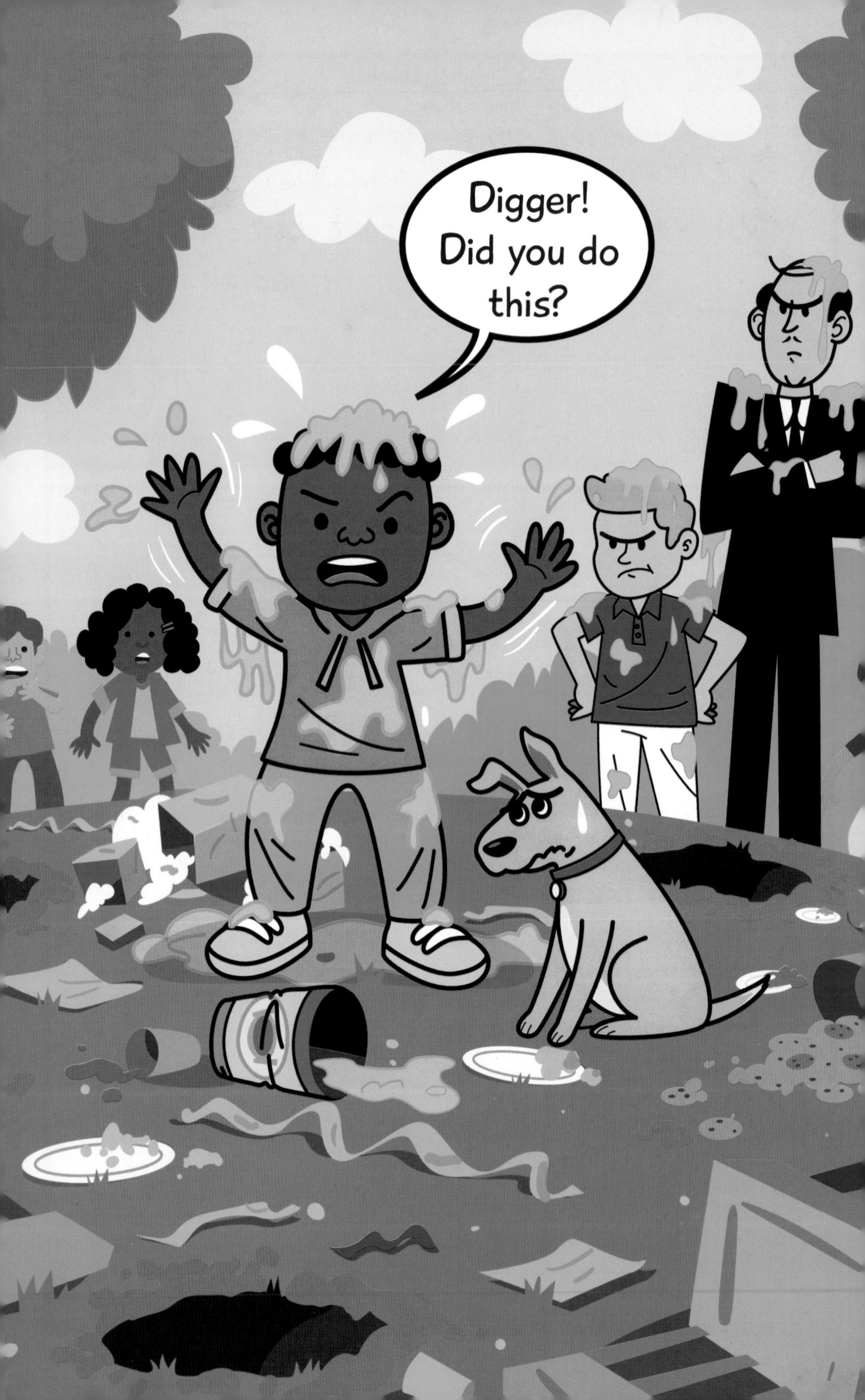
Digger! Did you do this?

Later at Kim's house...

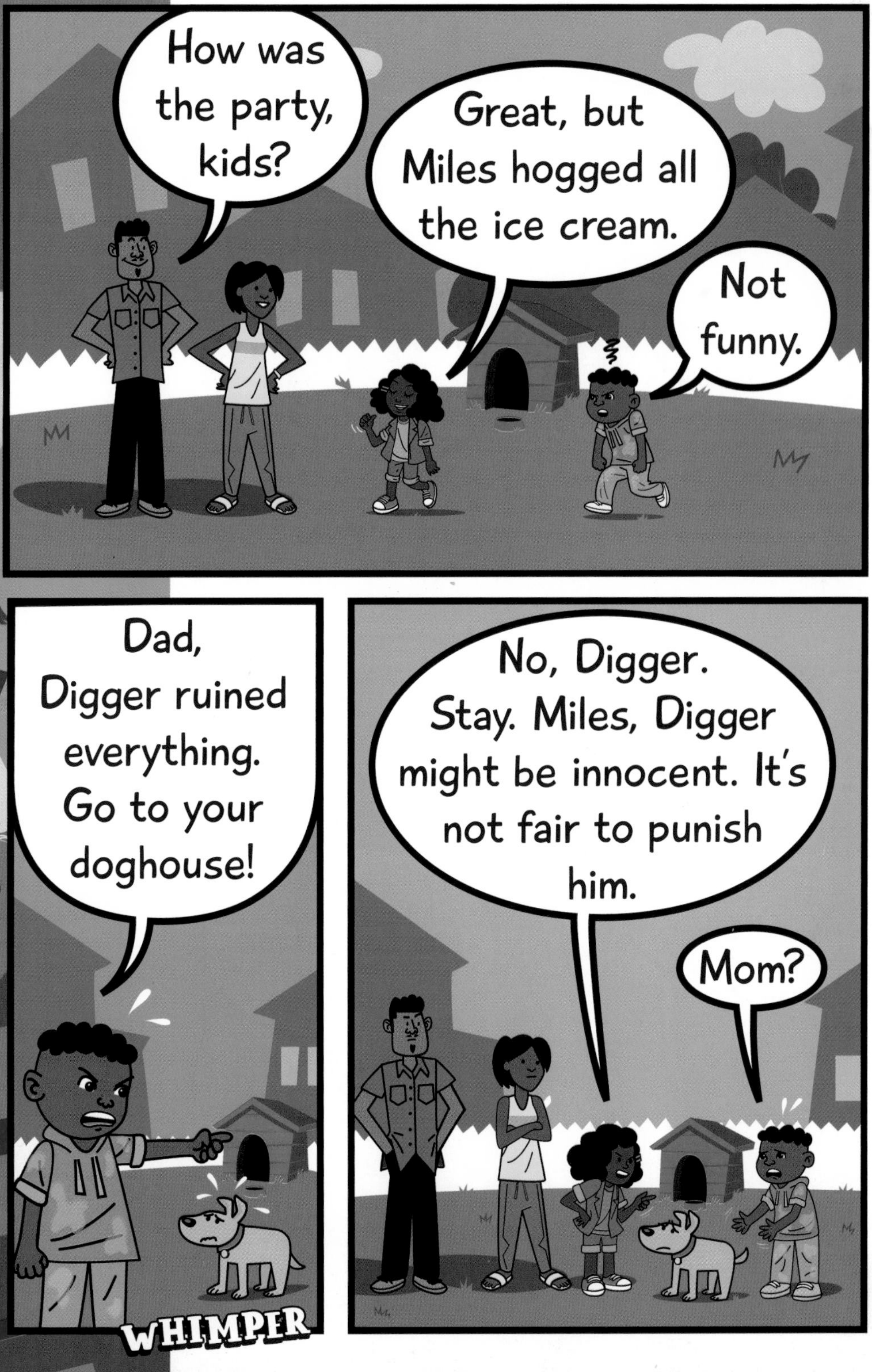
How was the party, kids?
Great, but Miles hogged all the ice cream.
Not funny.
Dad, Digger ruined everything. Go to your doghouse!
WHIMPER
No, Digger. Stay. Miles, Digger might be innocent. It's not fair to punish him.
Mom?

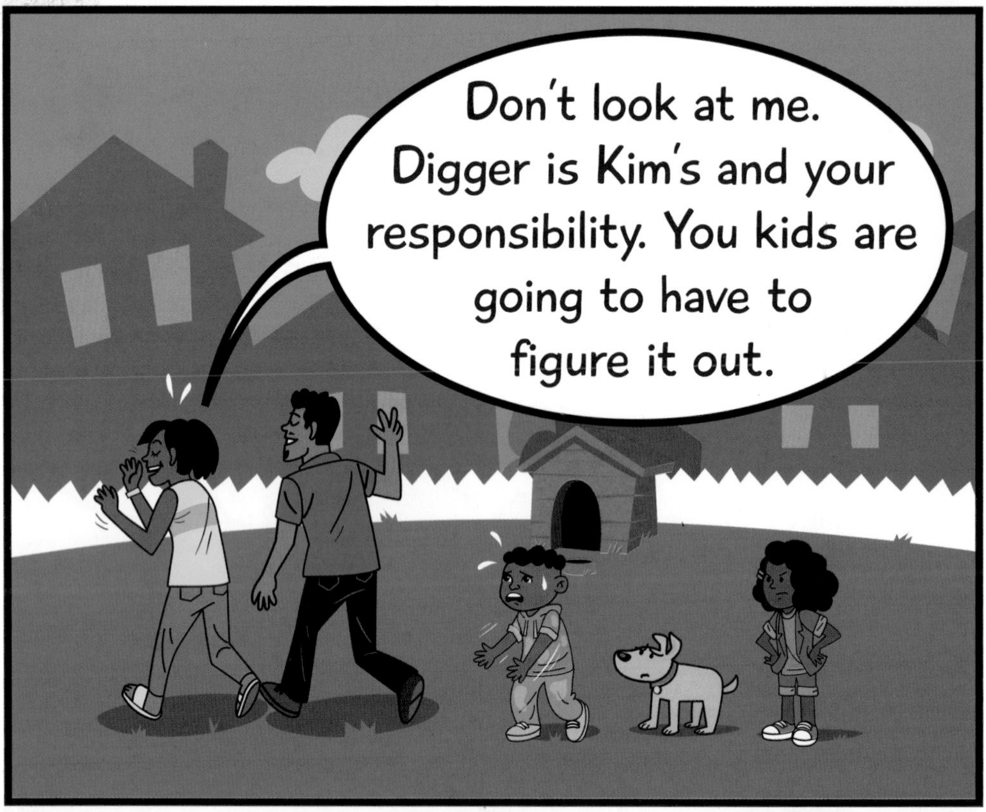
Don't look at me. Digger is Kim's and your responsibility. You kids are going to have to figure it out.

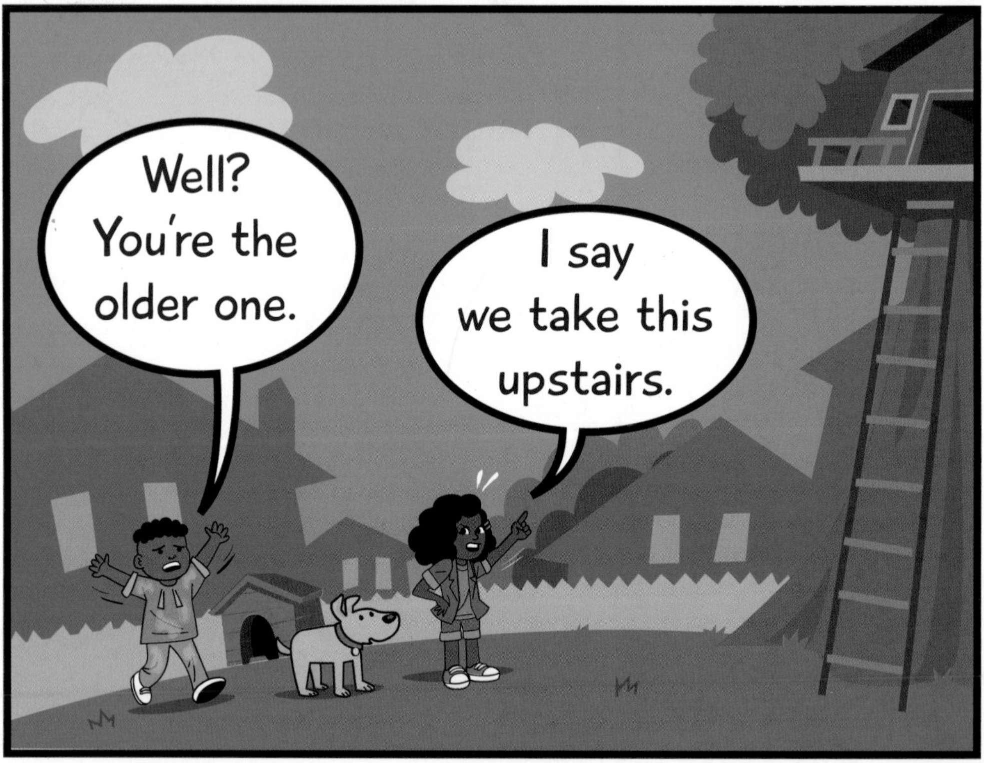
Well? You're the older one.
I say we take this upstairs.

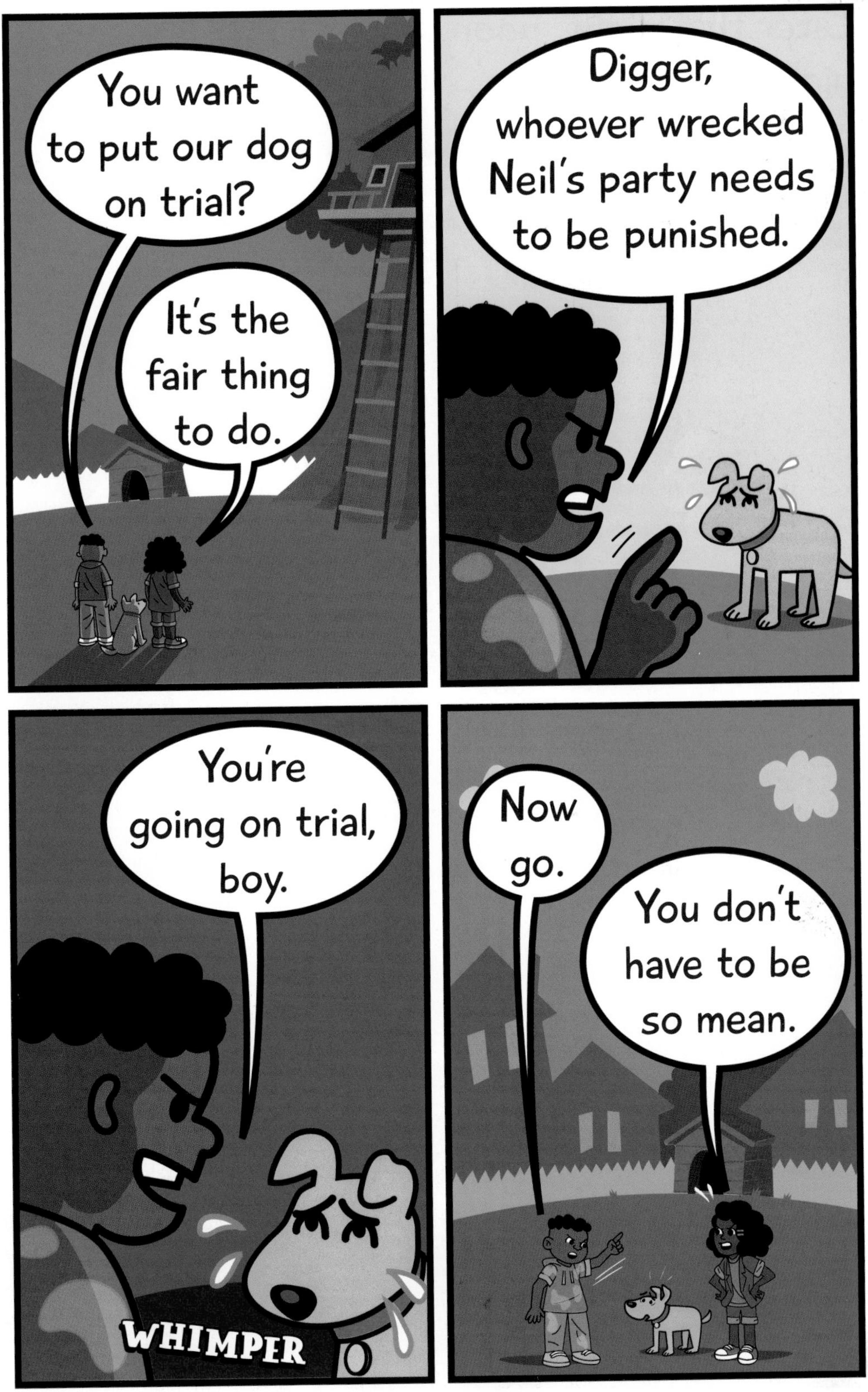
You want to put our dog on trial?
It's the fair thing to do.
Digger, whoever wrecked Neil's party needs to be punished.
You're going on trial, boy.
WHIMPER
Now go.
You don't have to be so mean.

Later that night, poor Digger has a nightmare...

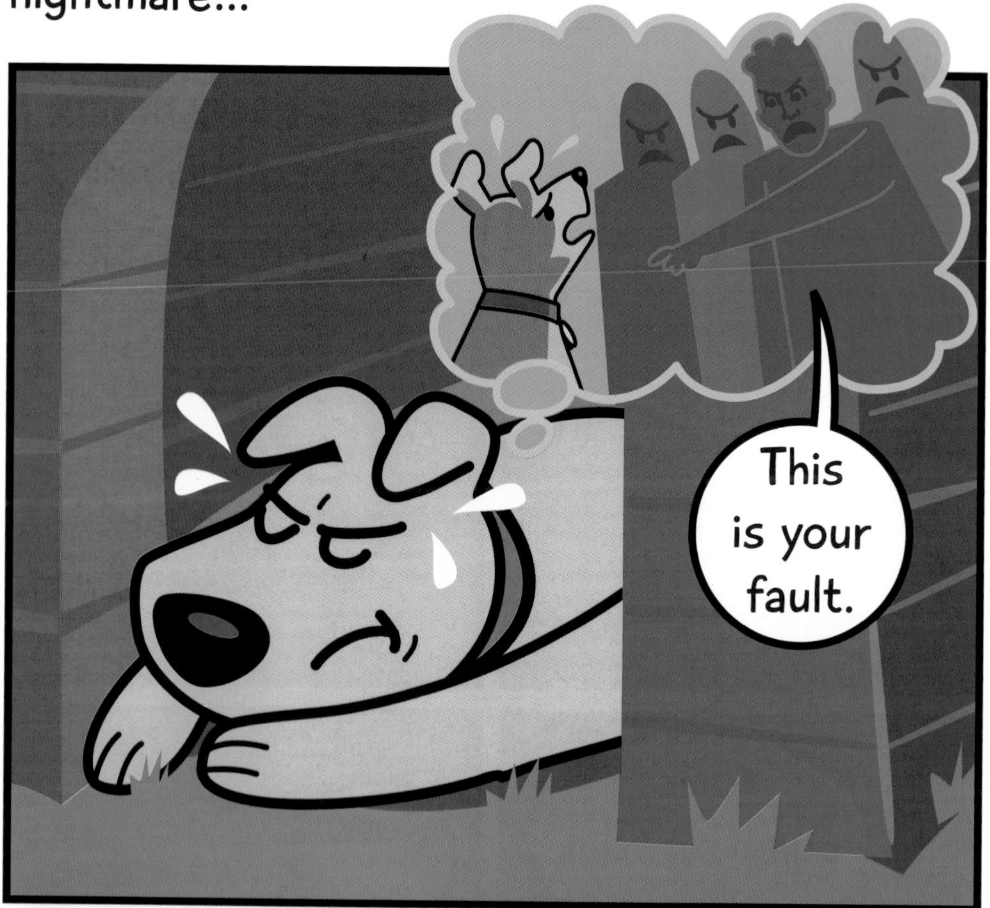
This is your fault.

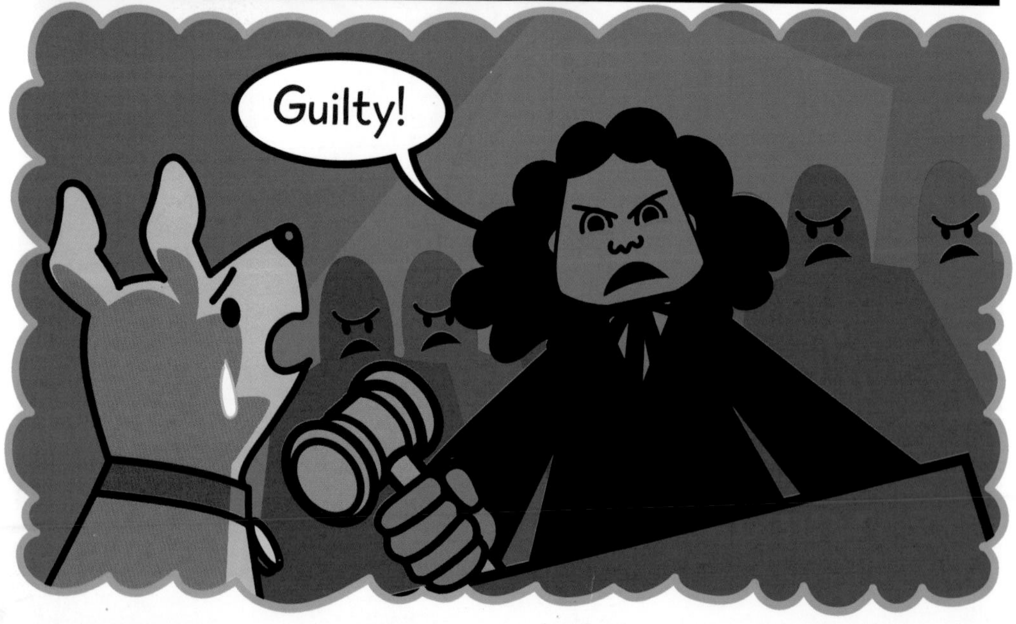
Guilty!

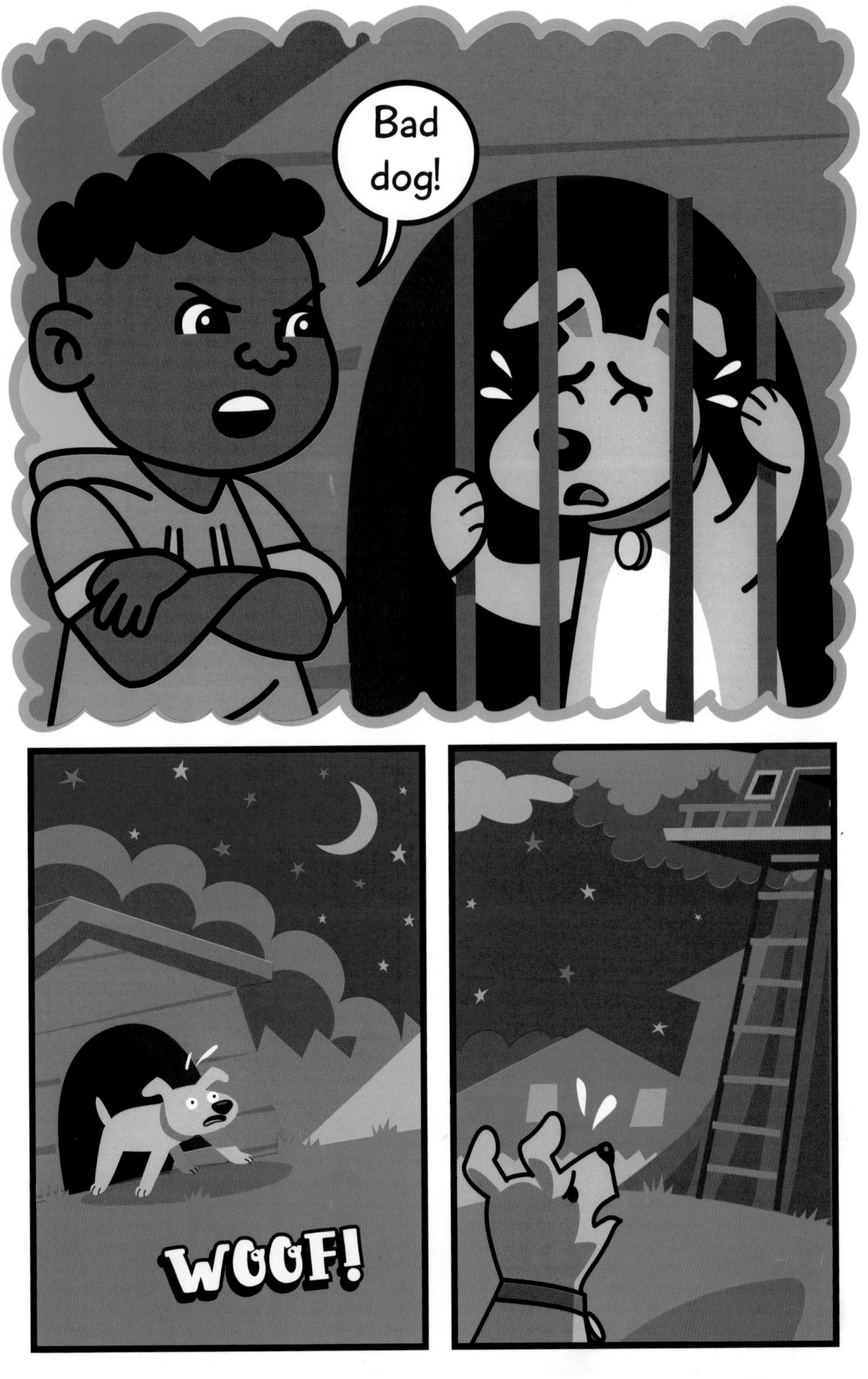
Bad dog!
WOOF!

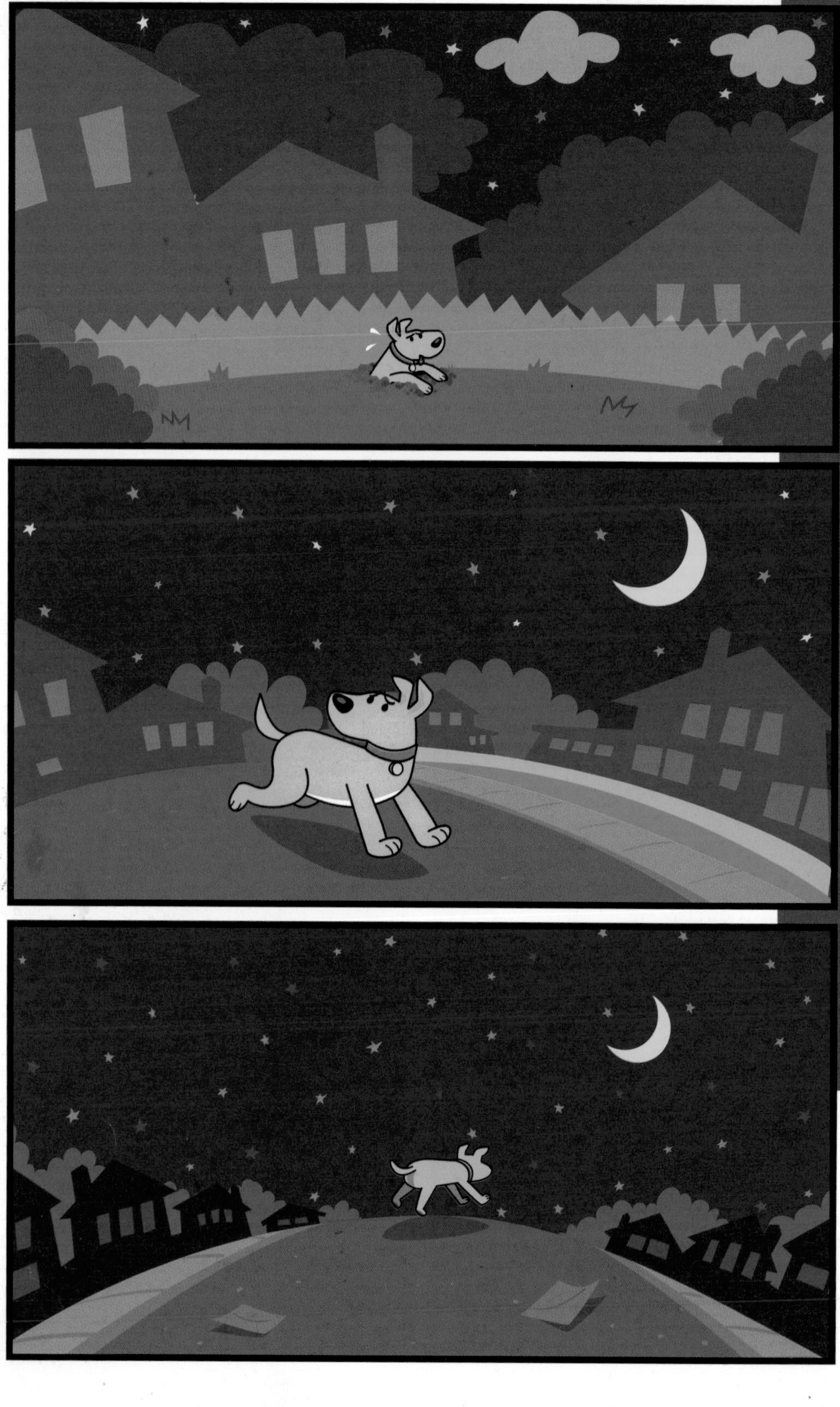

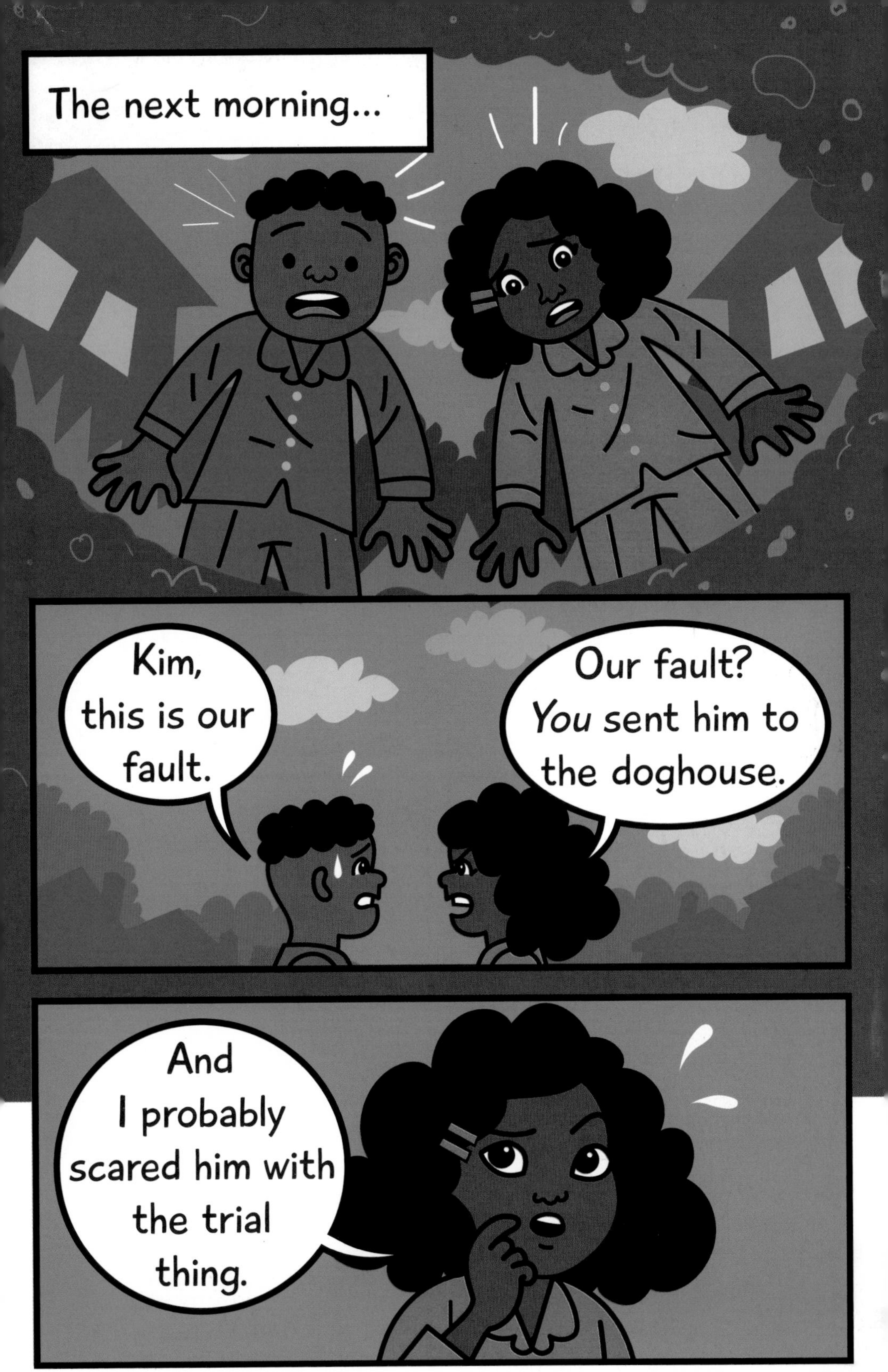
The next morning...
Kim, this is our fault.
Our fault? *You* sent him to the doghouse.
And I probably scared him with the trial thing.

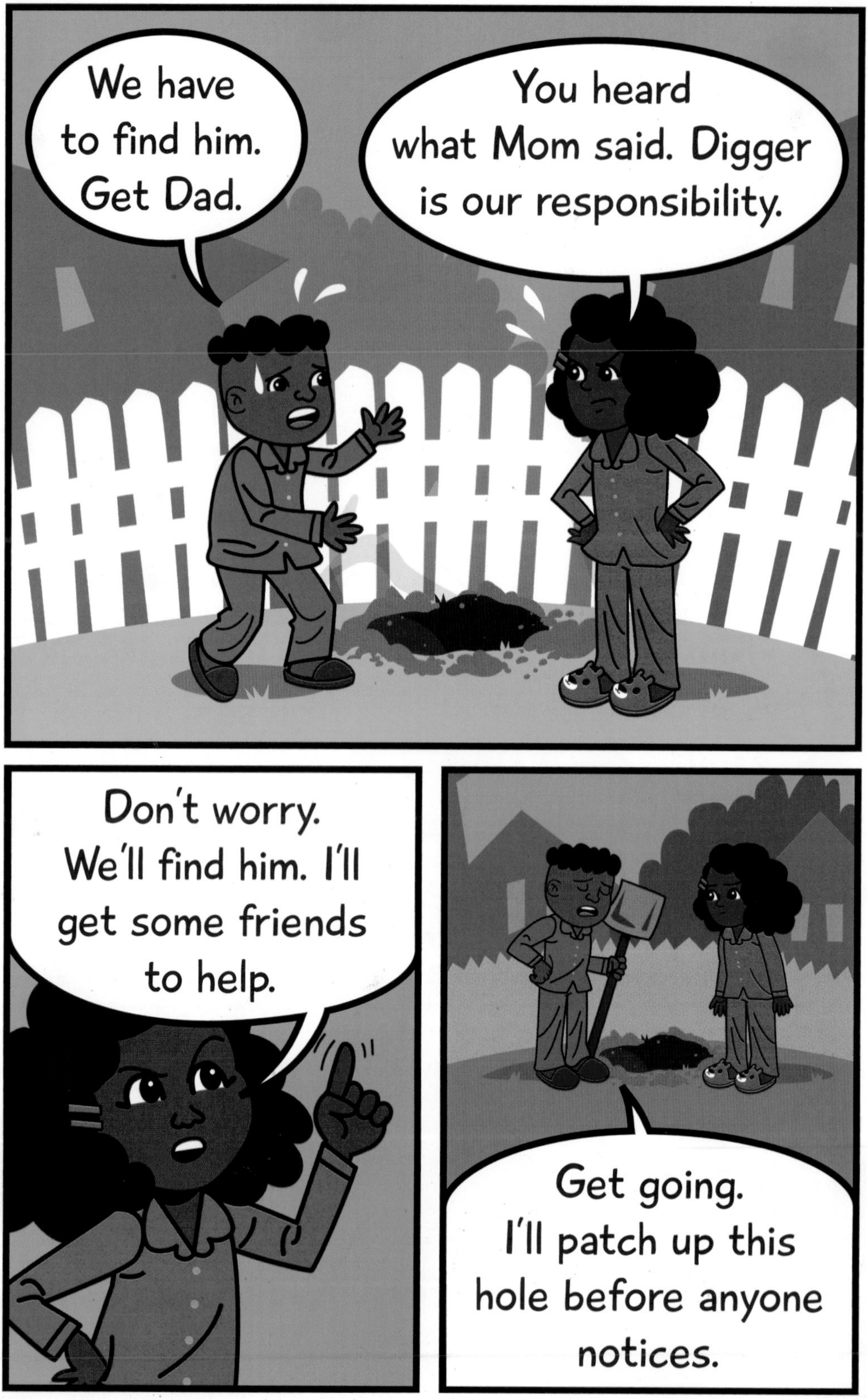
We have to find him. Get Dad.
You heard what Mom said. Digger is our responsibility.
Don't worry. We'll find him. I'll get some friends to help.
Get going. I'll patch up this hole before anyone notices.

Kim and her friends search Fairville, one street after the other...

from the school to the shopping mall...

past the church and the courthouse...

beyond the farms, all the way to the edge of town.

Miles and Miguel stop at Neil's house to ask for help.

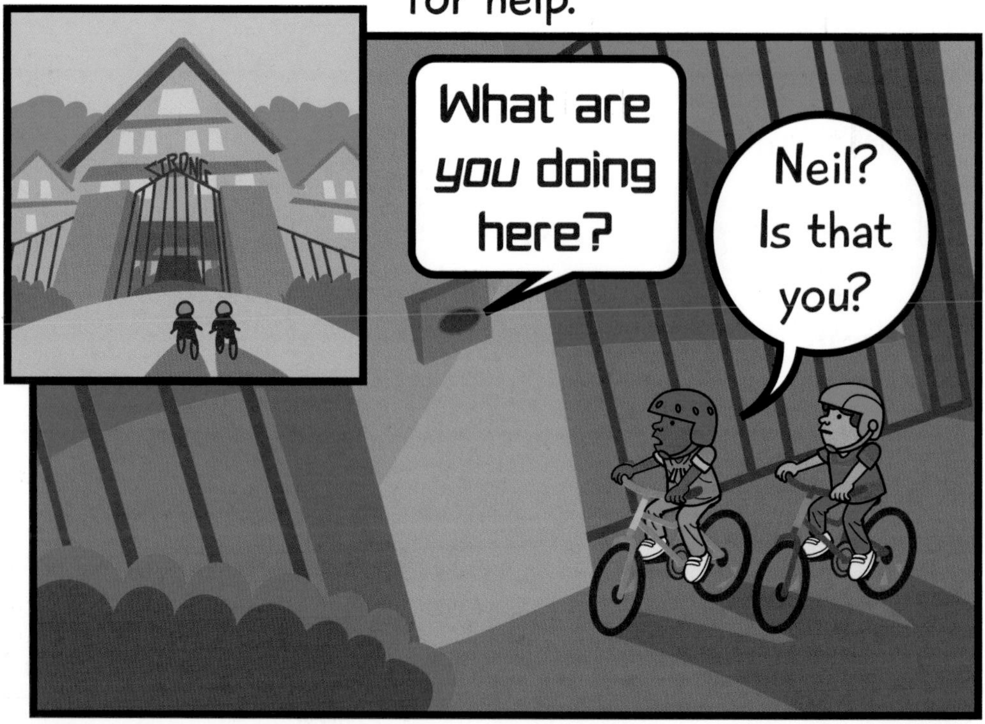
STRONG
What are *you* doing here?
Neil? Is that you?

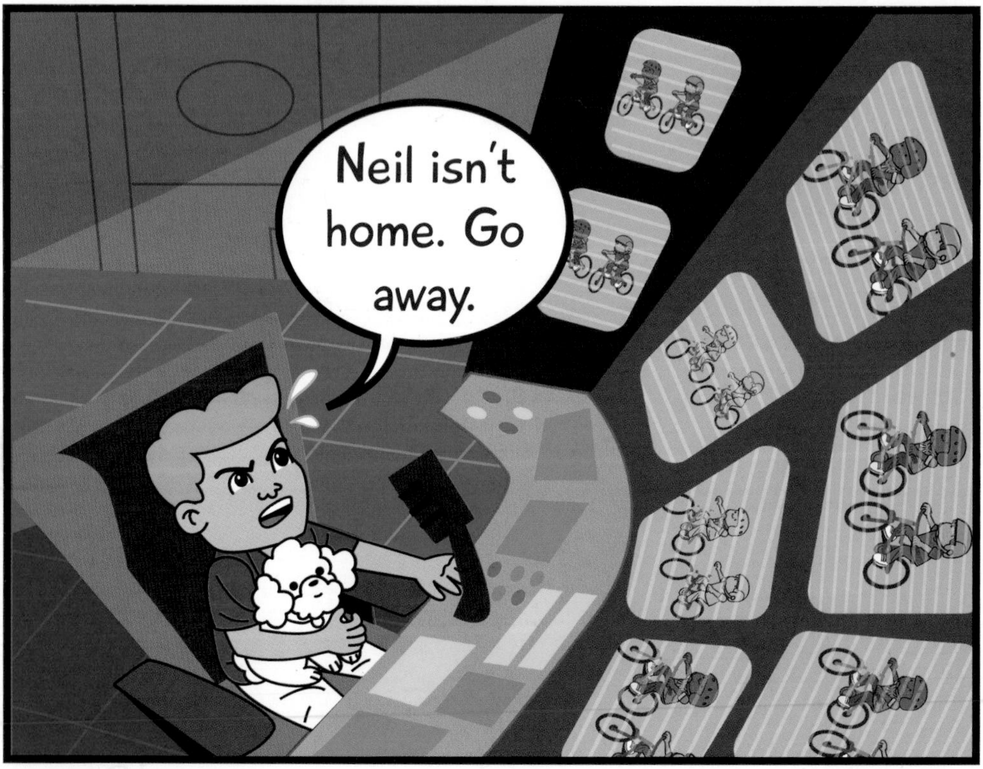
Neil isn't home. Go away.

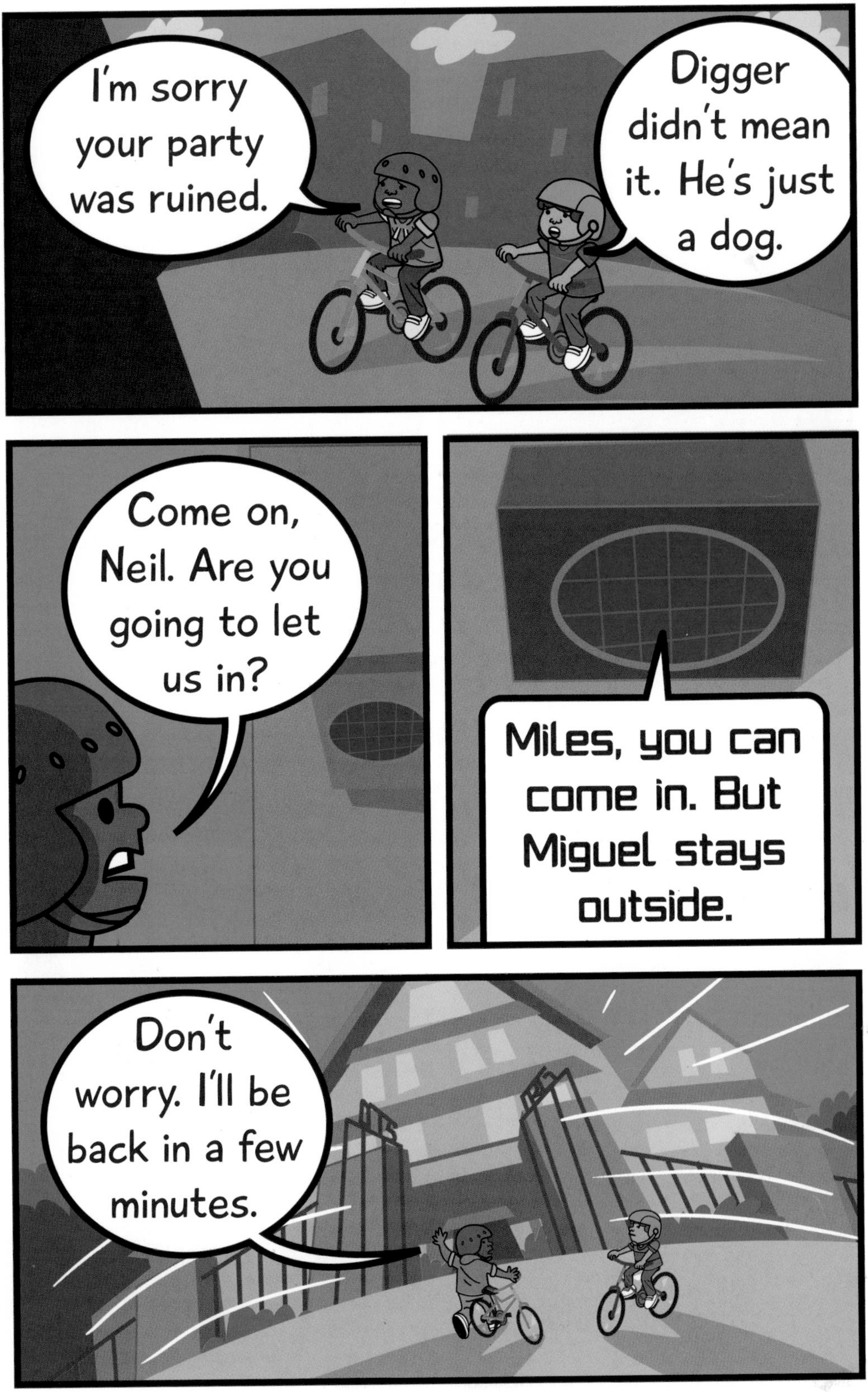
I'm sorry your party was ruined.
Digger didn't mean it. He's just a dog.
Come on, Neil. Are you going to let us in?
Miles, you can come in. But Miguel stays outside.
Don't worry. I'll be back in a few minutes.

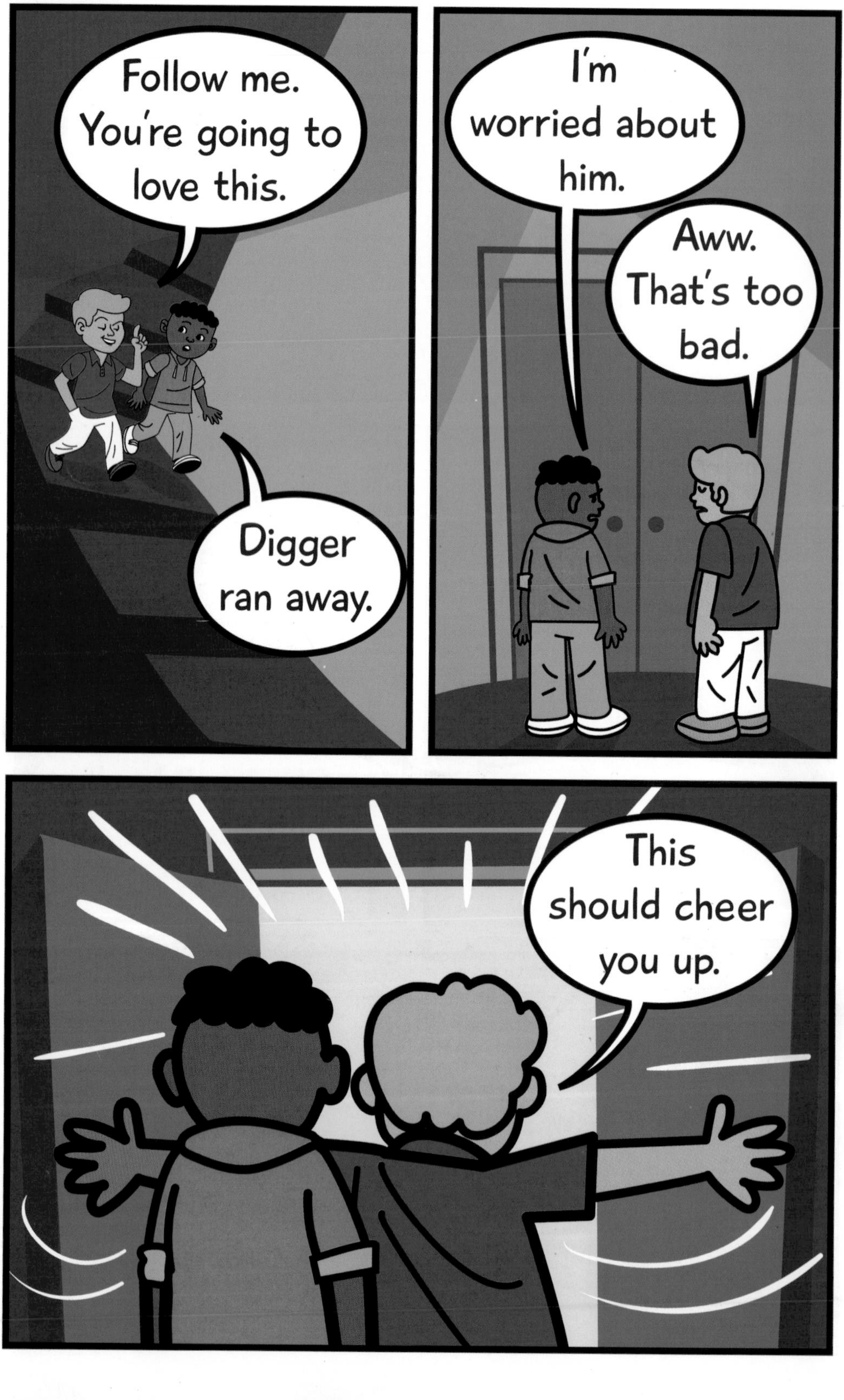
Follow me. You're going to love this.
Digger ran away.
I'm worried about him.
Aww. That's too bad.
This should cheer you up.

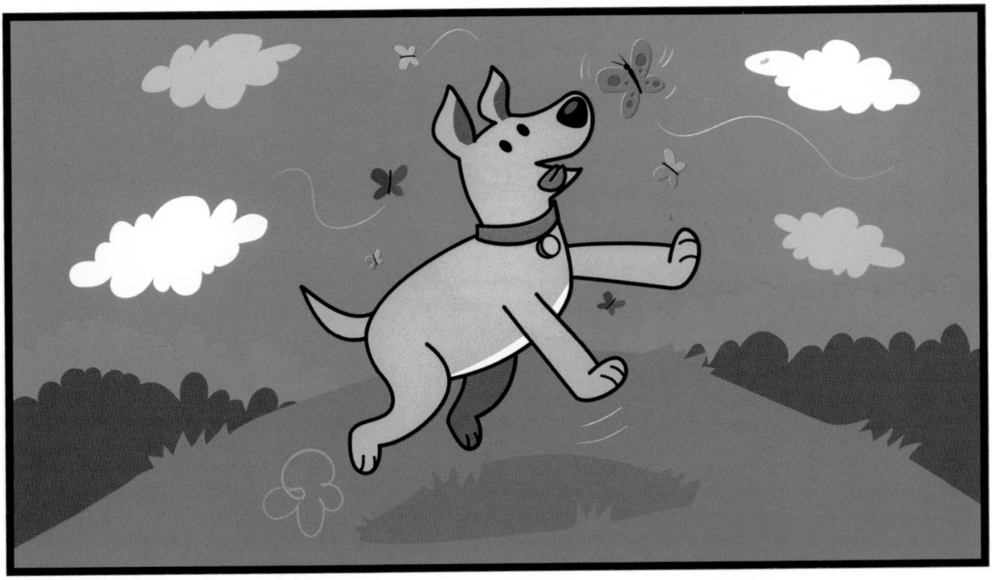

It looks like Digger is enjoying a little adventure away from home.

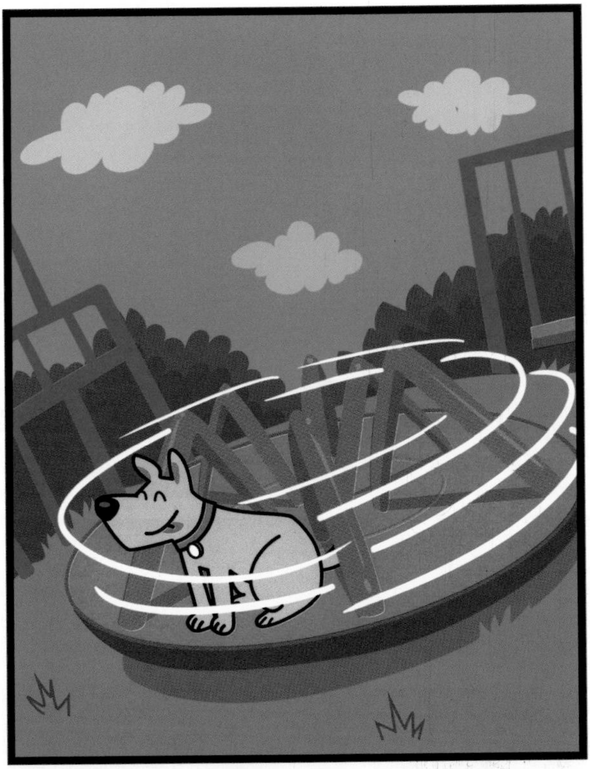

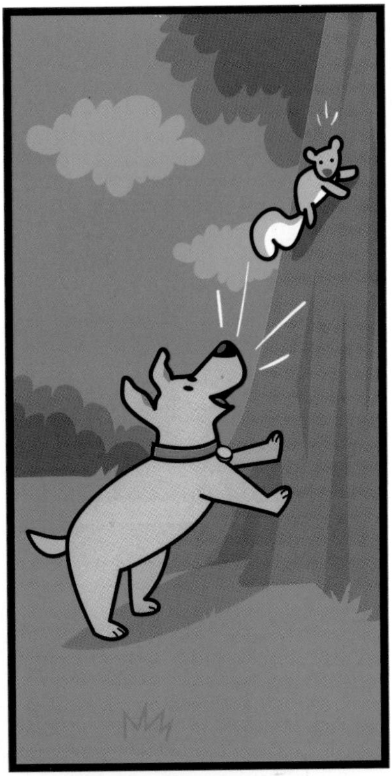

Digger thinks the playground and chasing squirrels is a lot more fun than the Kids' Court.

After a long day of searching...

A little adventure is always fun...

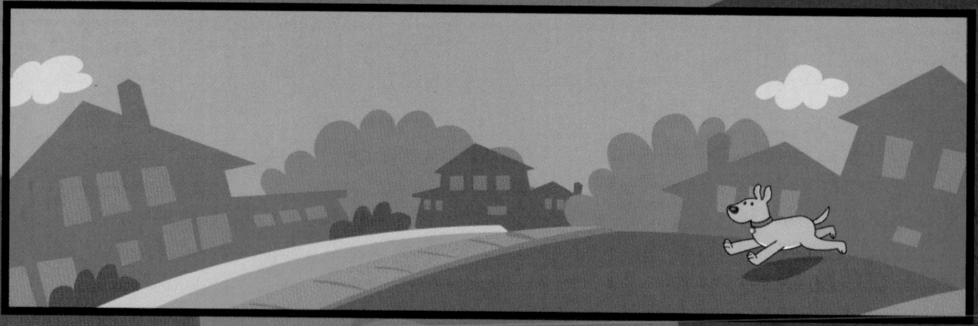

...but back to Fairville, Digger goes.

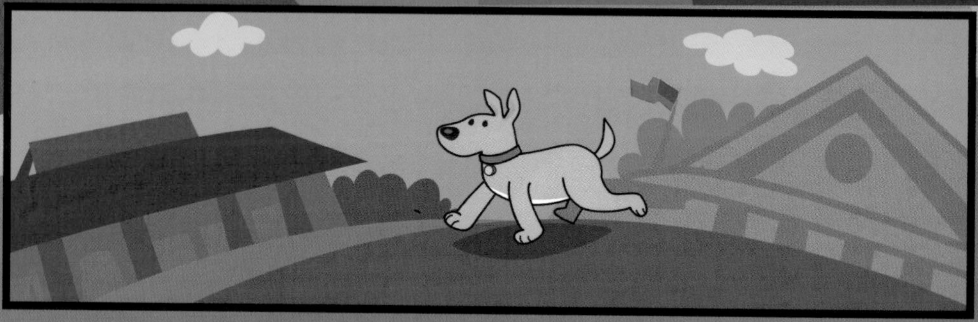

Because even a dog knows...

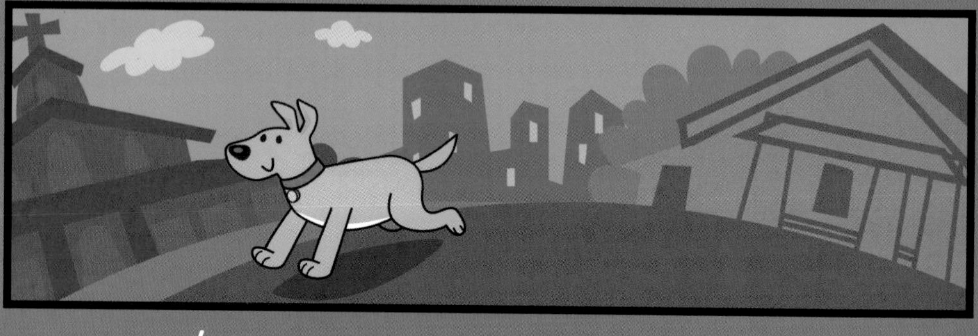

...you can't run away from your problems.

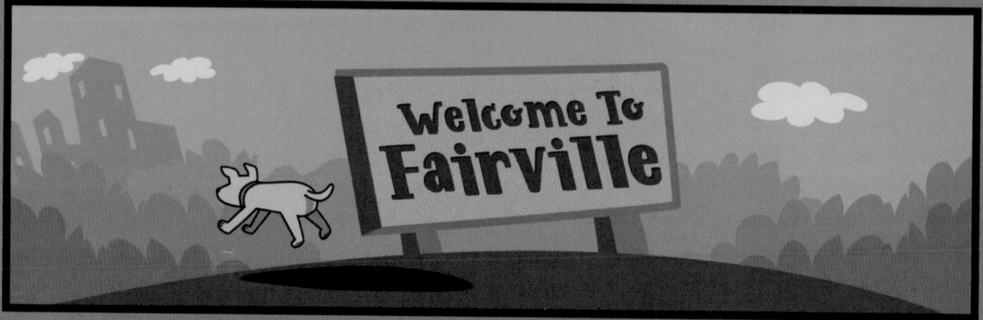
Welcome To
Fairville

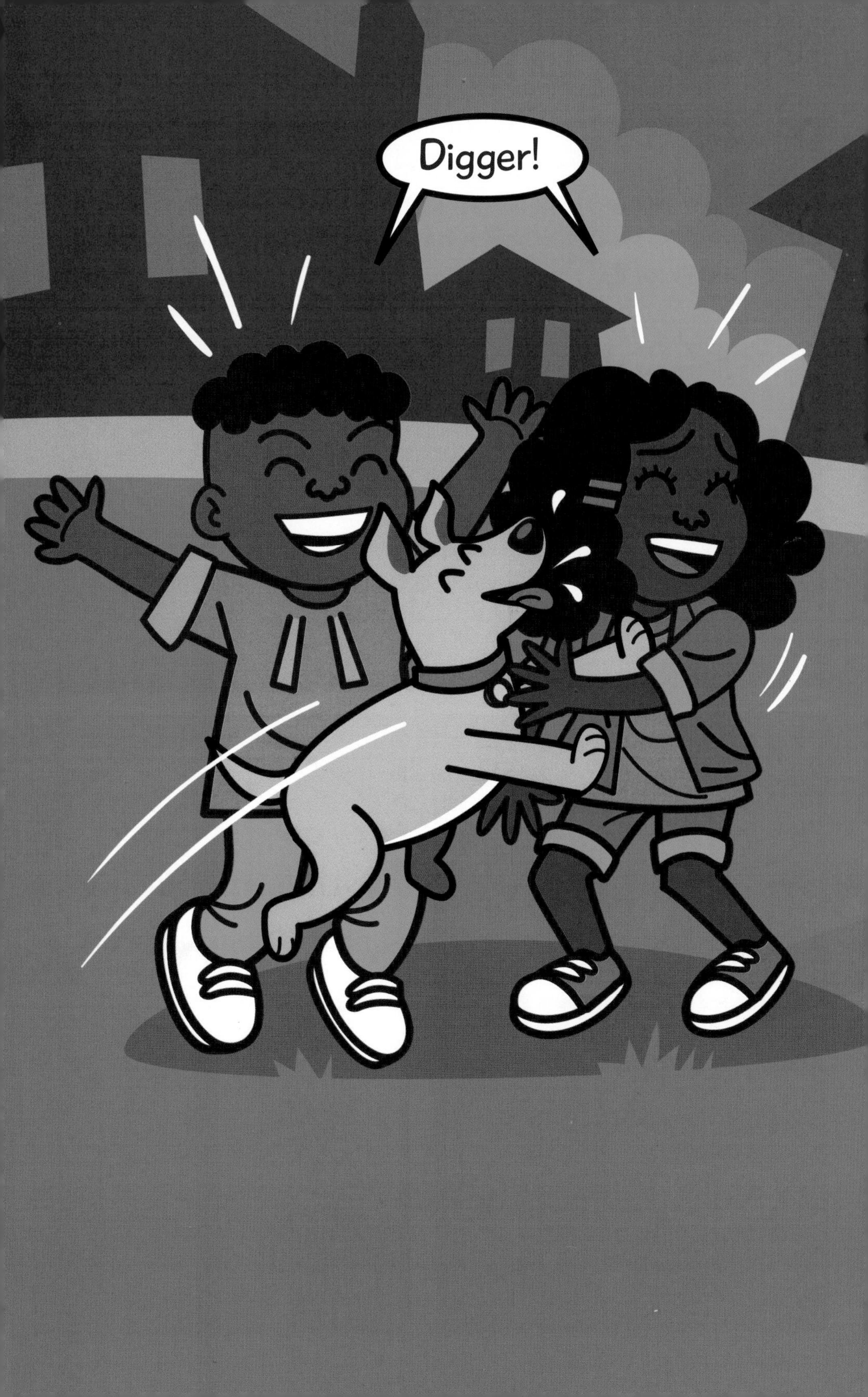
Digger!

At last, a dog will have his day in court.

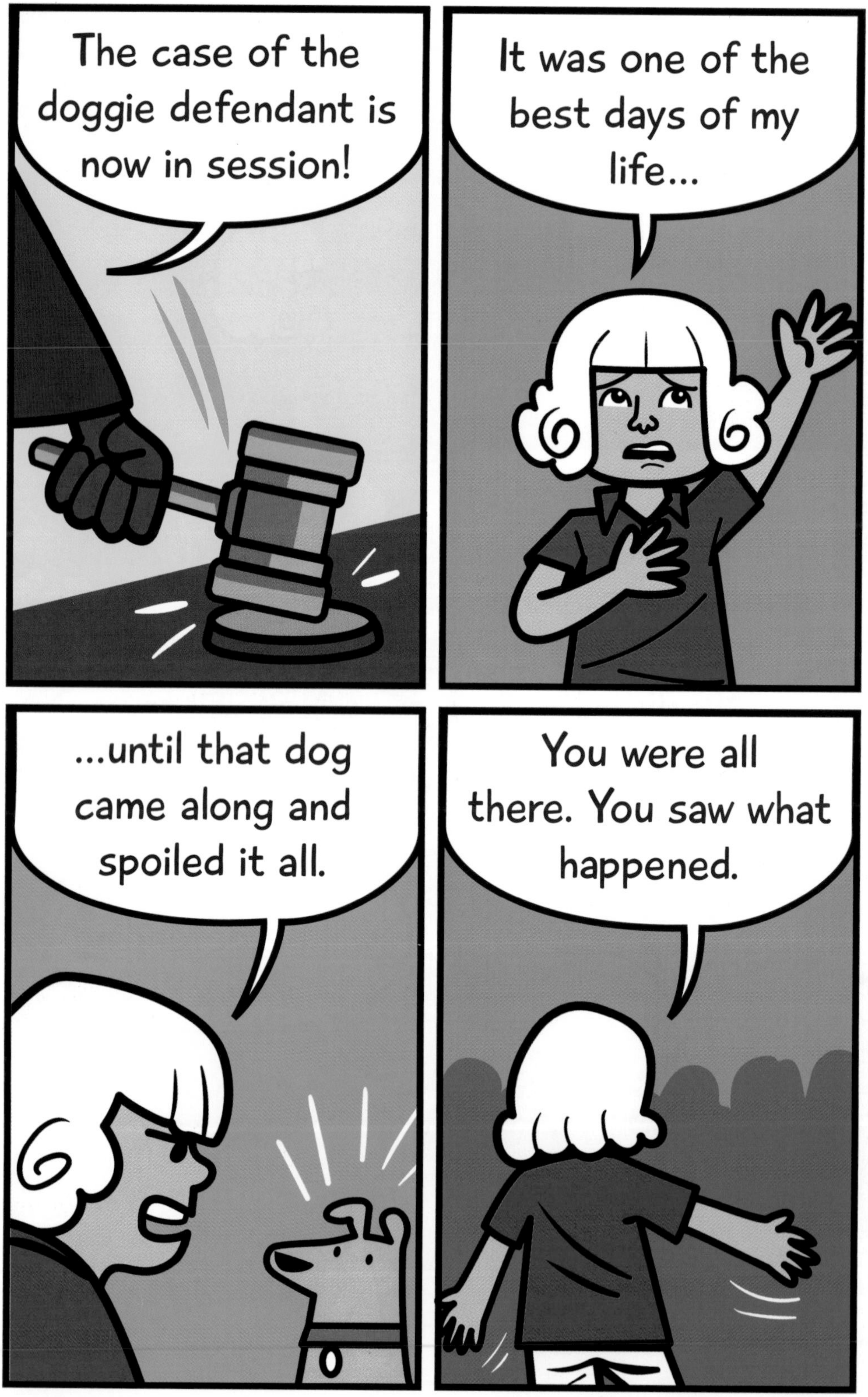
The case of the doggie defendant is now in session!
It was one of the best days of my life...
...until that dog came along and spoiled it all.
You were all there. You saw what happened.

Neil weaves a story of what he thinks happened that day...

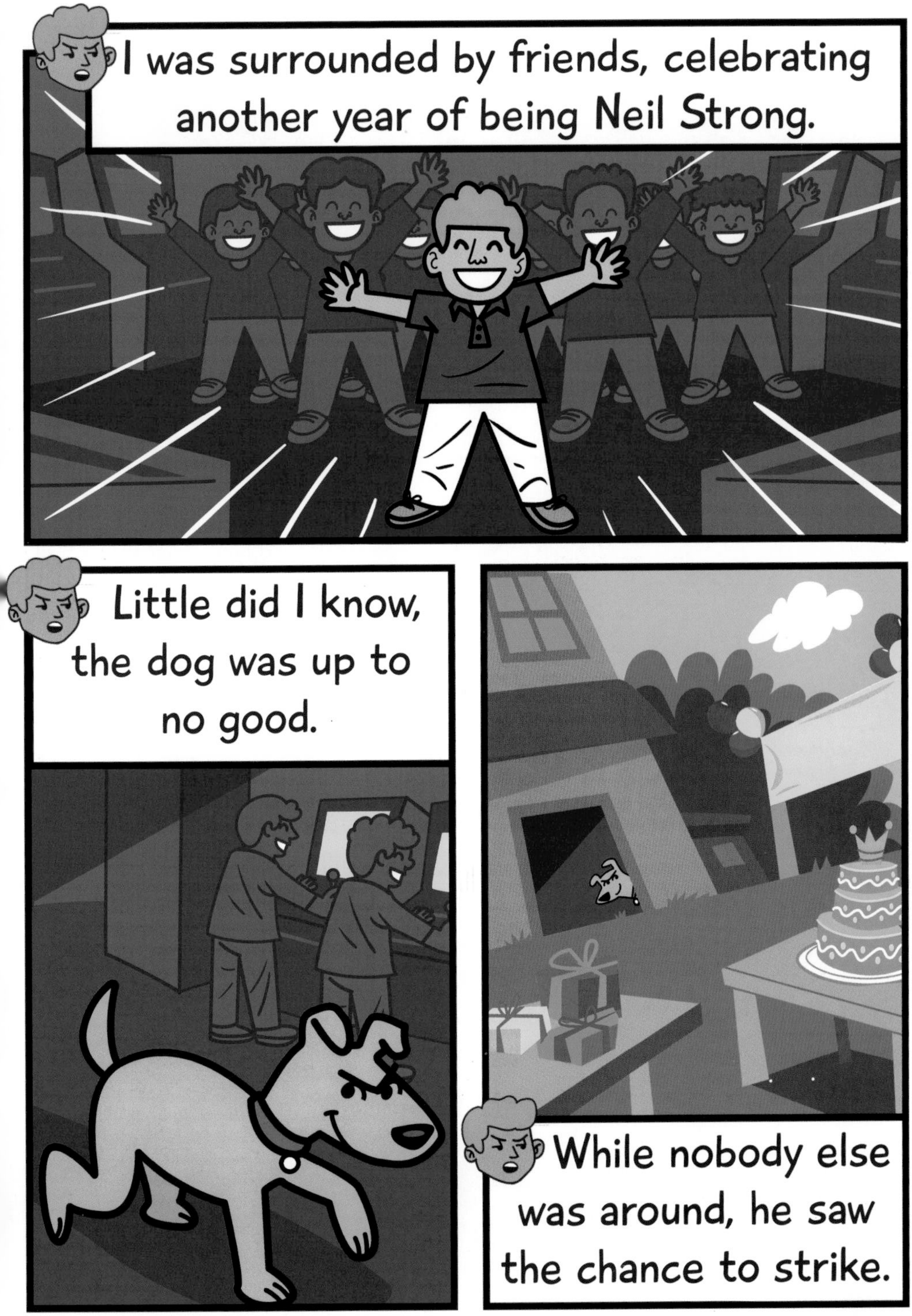
I was surrounded by friends, celebrating another year of being Neil Strong.
Little did I know, the dog was up to no good.
While nobody else was around, he saw the chance to strike.

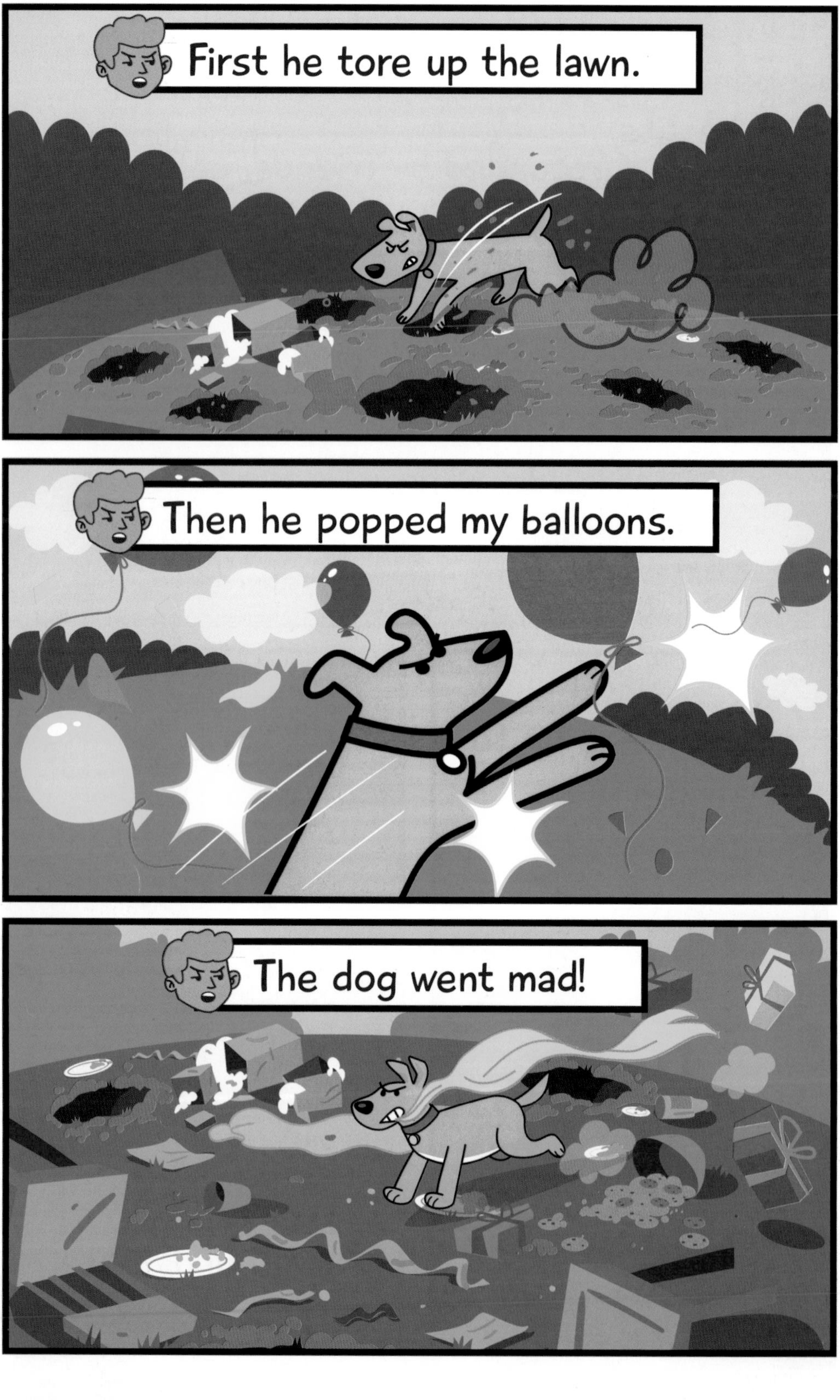
First he tore up the lawn.
Then he popped my balloons.
The dog went mad!

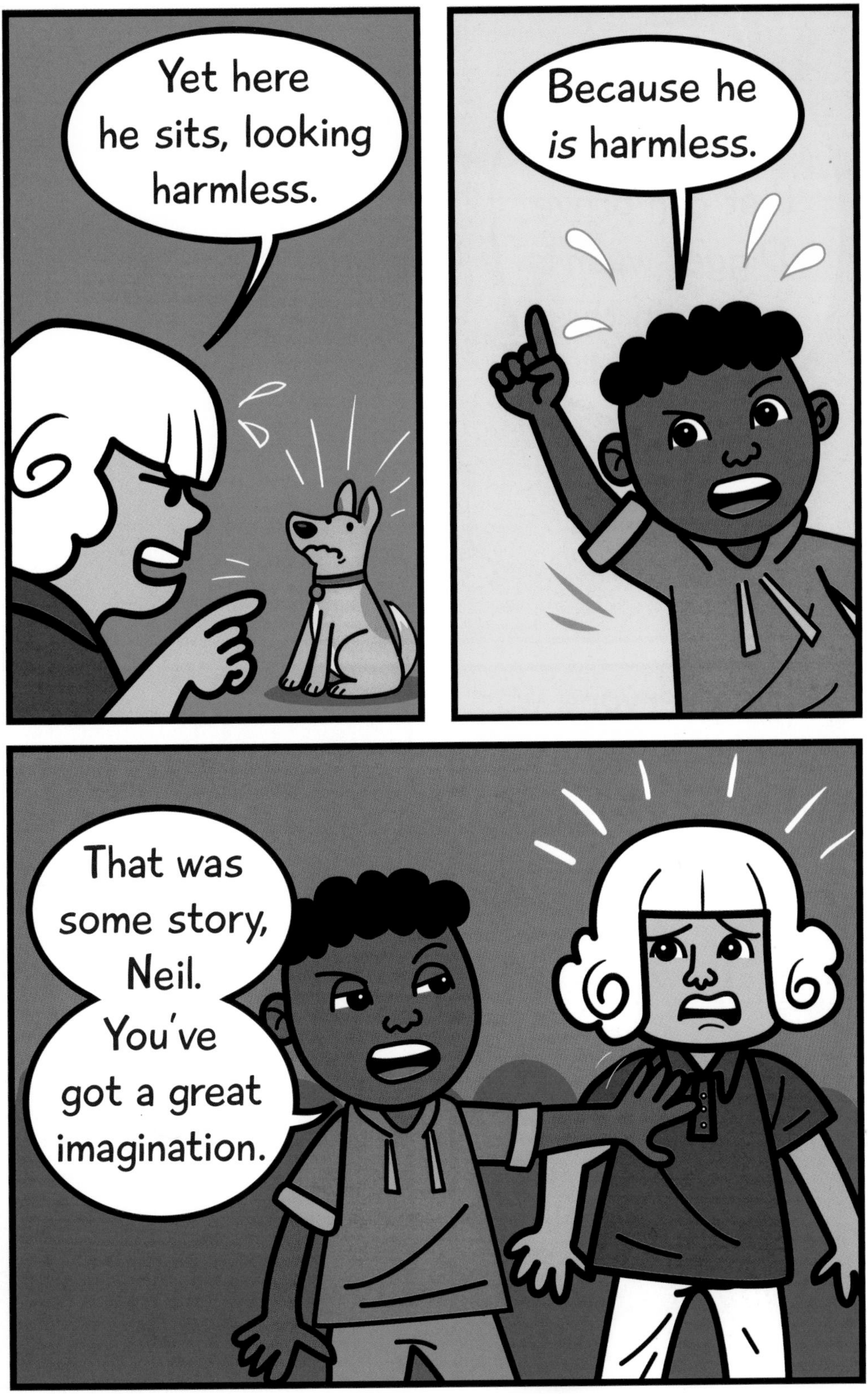
Yet here he *sits*, looking harmless.
Because he *is* harmless.
That was some story, Neil.
You've got a great imagination.

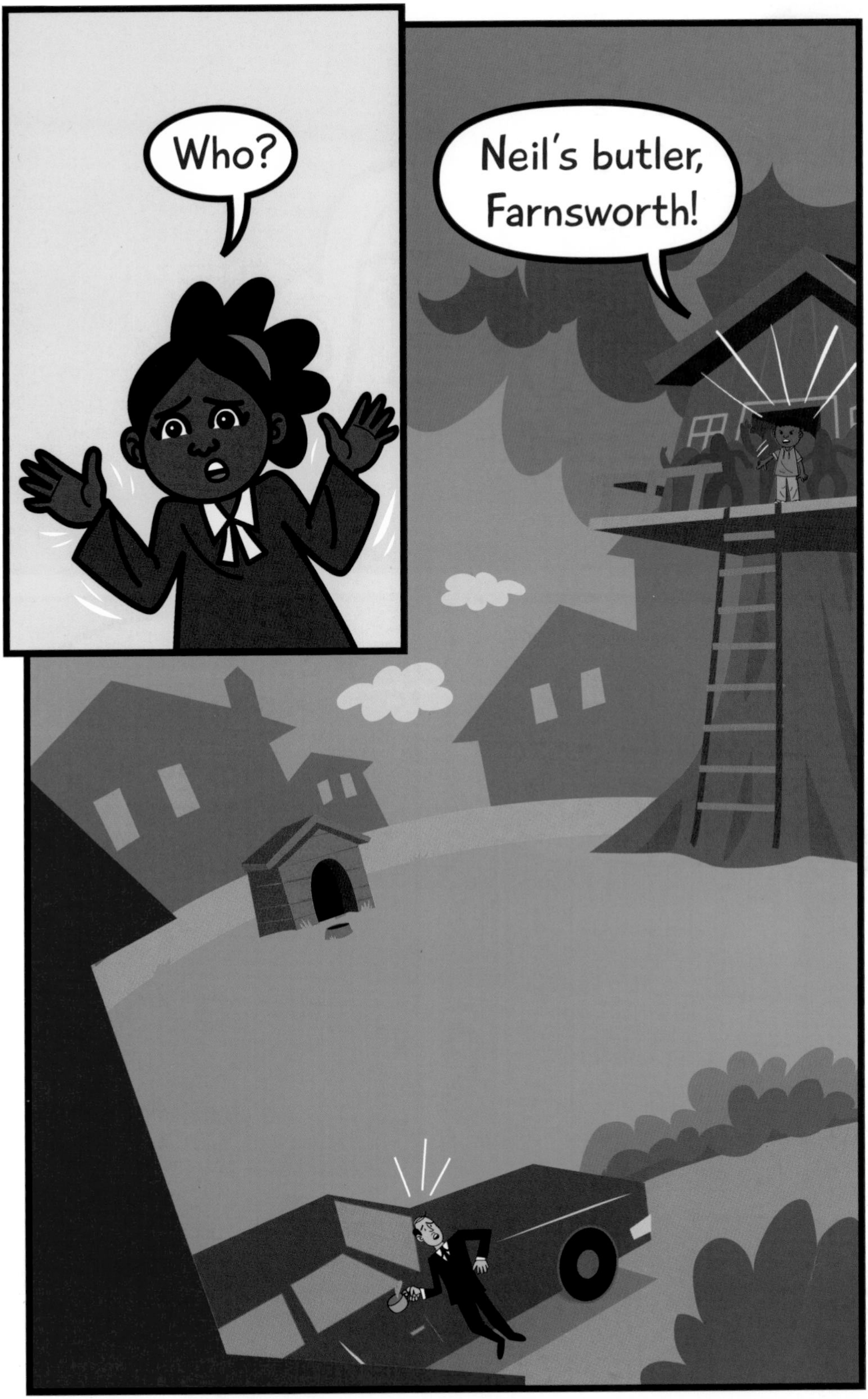
Who?
Neil's butler, Farnsworth!

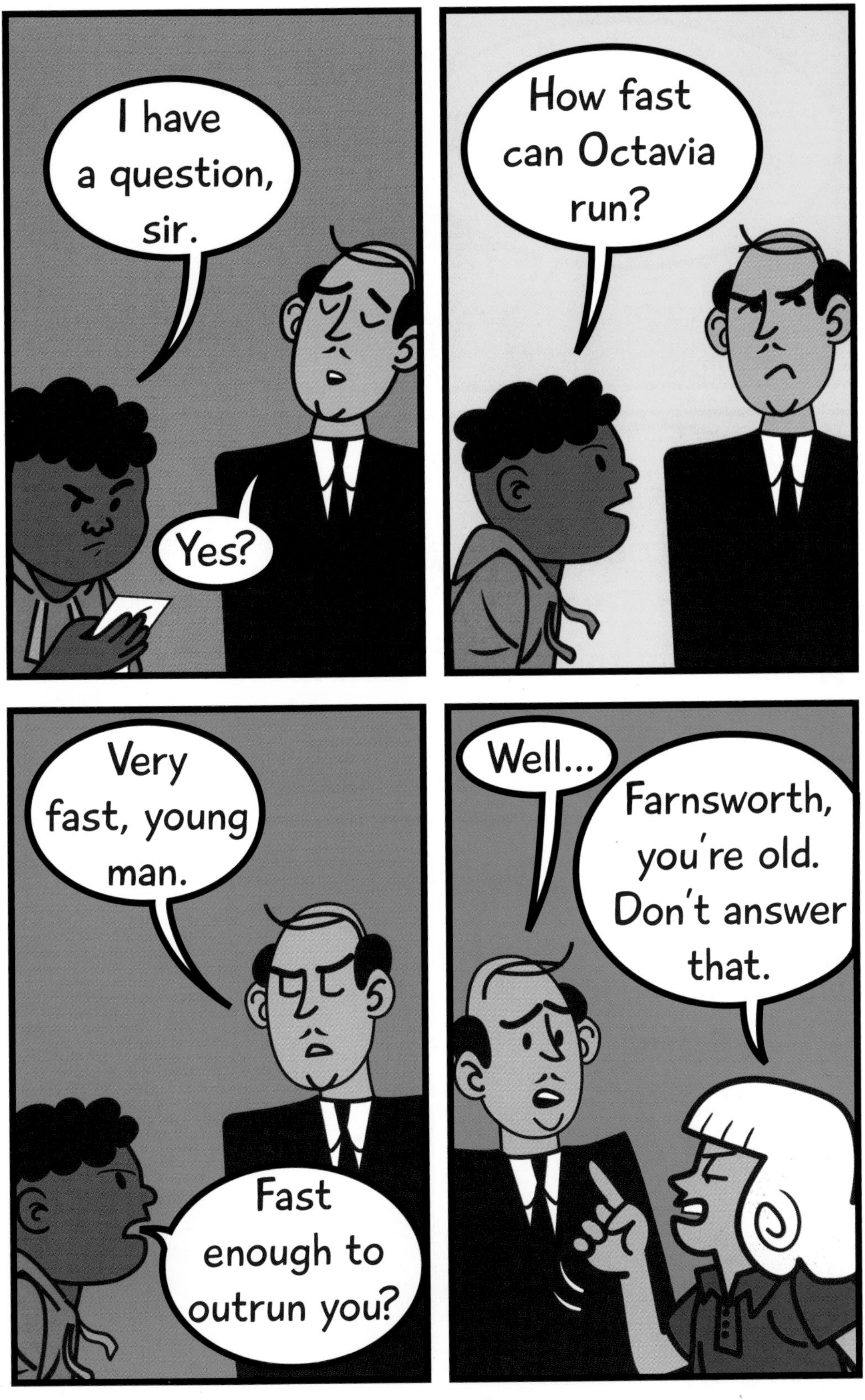
I have a question, sir.
Yes?
How fast can Octavia run?
Very fast, young man.
Fast enough to outrun you?
Well...
Farnsworth, you're old. Don't answer that.

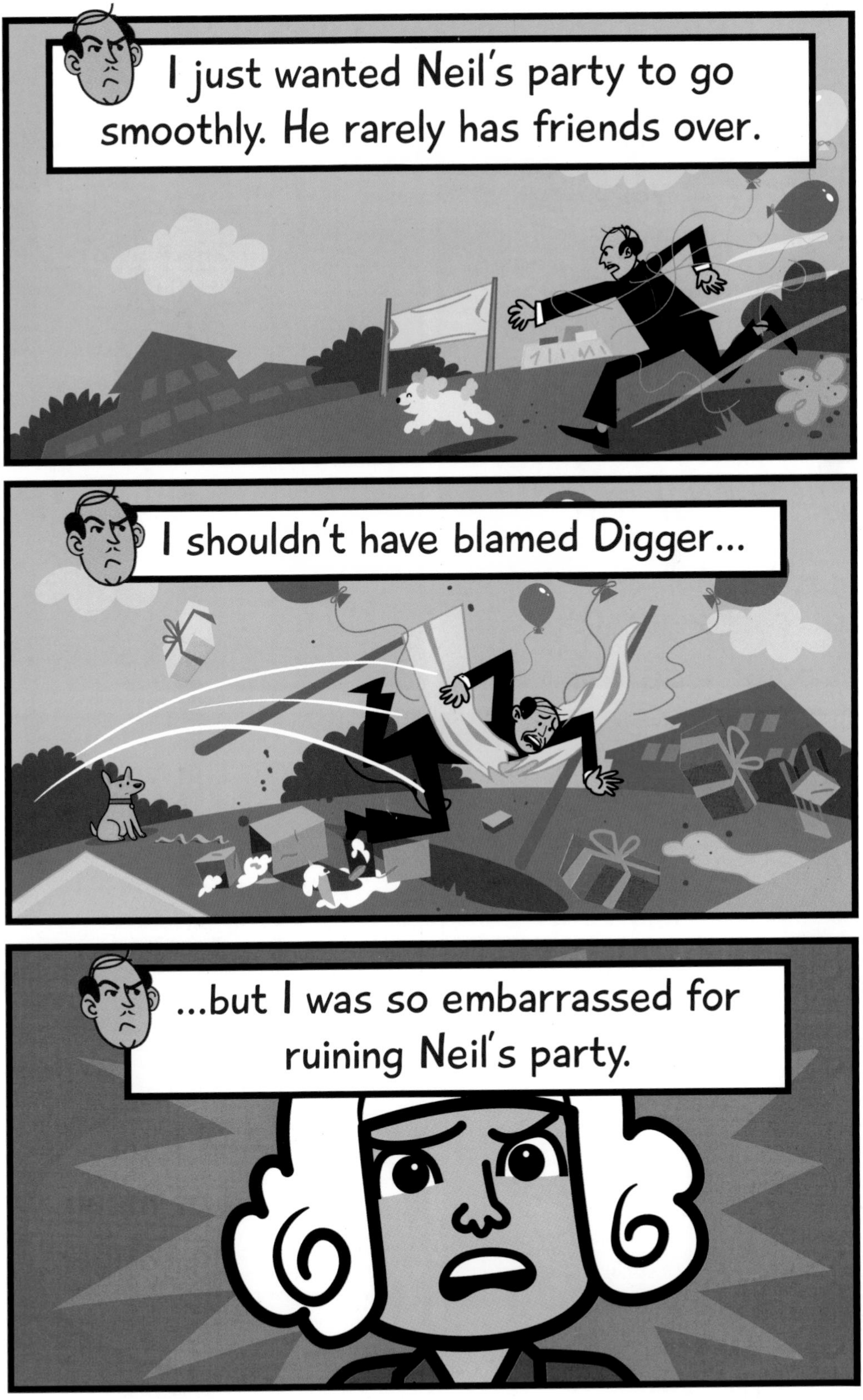
I just wanted Neil's party to go smoothly. He rarely has friends over.
I shouldn't have blamed Digger...
...but I was so embarrassed for ruining Neil's party.

After court Neil decides to take his friends for a ride.

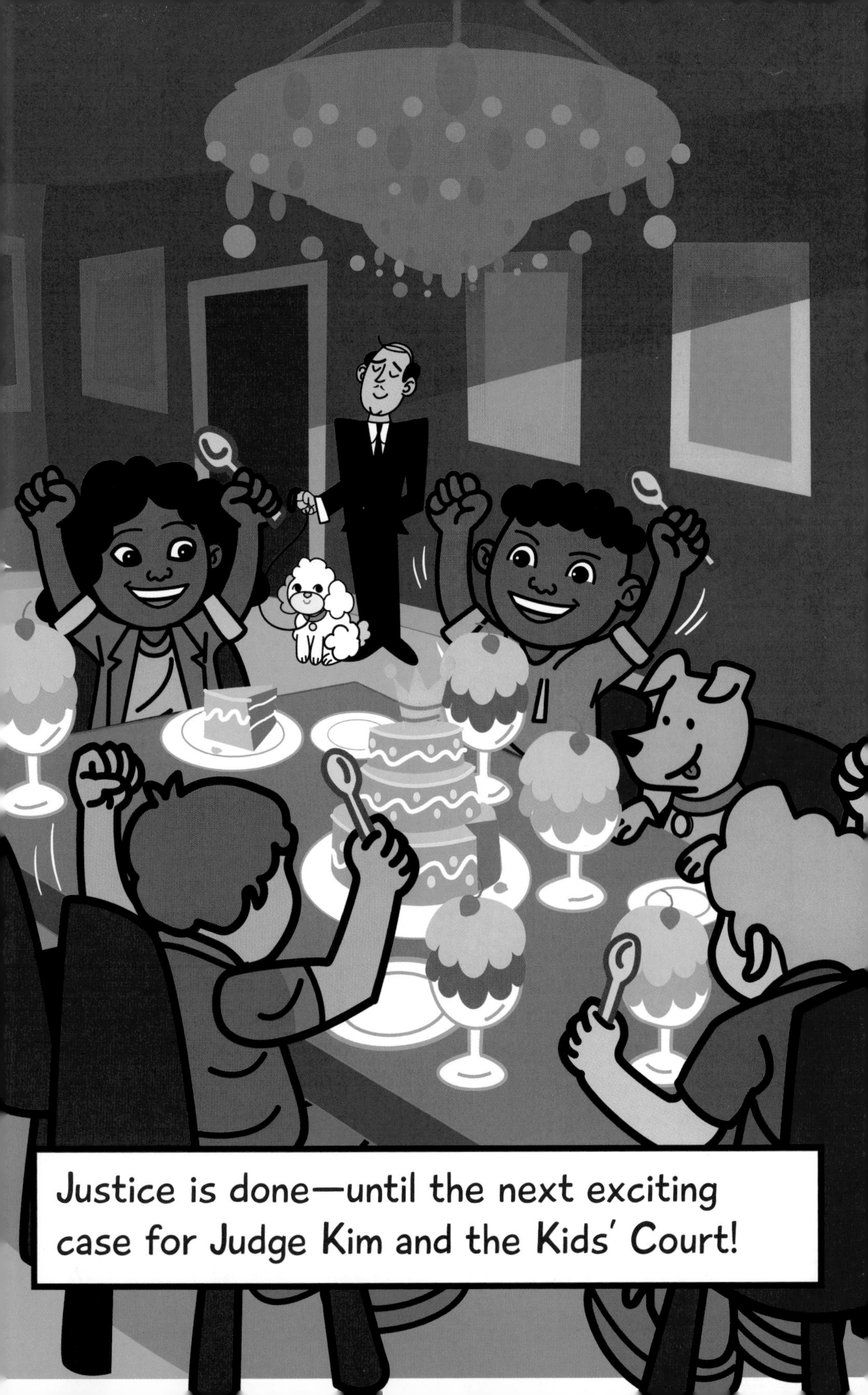
Justice is done—until the next exciting case for Judge Kim and the Kids' Court!

GLOSSARY

<u>case</u>: a disagreement between two people or groups that is decided in court.

<u>court</u>: a place where a judge listens to and decides on cases.

<u>defendant</u>: a person who is brought to court because they are accused of doing something wrong.

<u>evidence</u>: information presented in court to help a judge understand a case.

<u>judge</u>: a person who listens to cases and decides who is right and who is wrong.

<u>justice</u>: when a proper punishment or fair treatment is given by a judge.

<u>lawyer</u>: a person who helps people present their side in court. Then the judge can decide who wins the case.

<u>trial</u>: when a case is brought to court to decide whether or not a person has broken the law.

<u>witness</u>: a person who saw something happen that is related to a case.

Note to readers: Some of these words may have more than one definition. The definitions above match how these words are used in this book.